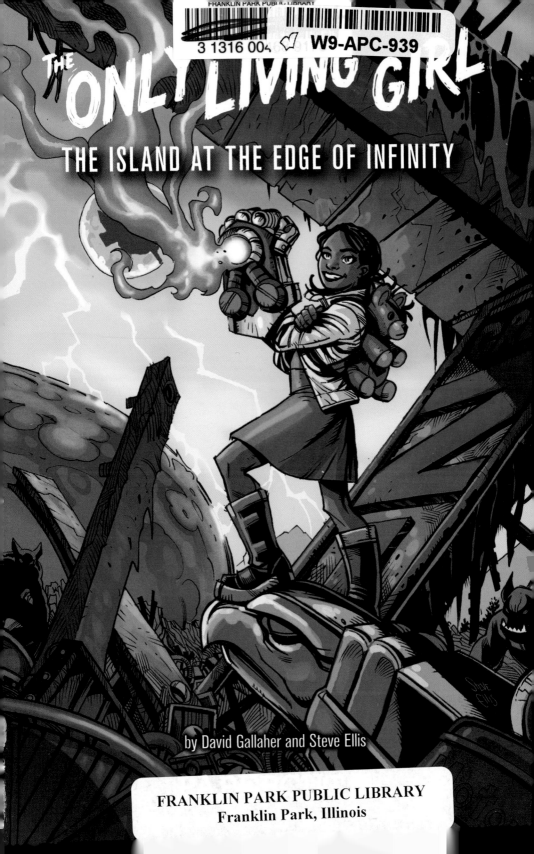

THE ONLY LIVING GIRL

THE ISLAND AT THE EDGE OF INFINITY

by David Gallaher and Steve Ellis

To my wonderful family, who put up with an artist who is always on crazy deadlines. Thanks for the support, Mila, Jacob and Luna! –Steve

To my family, for their endless support, compassion, and inspiration! –David

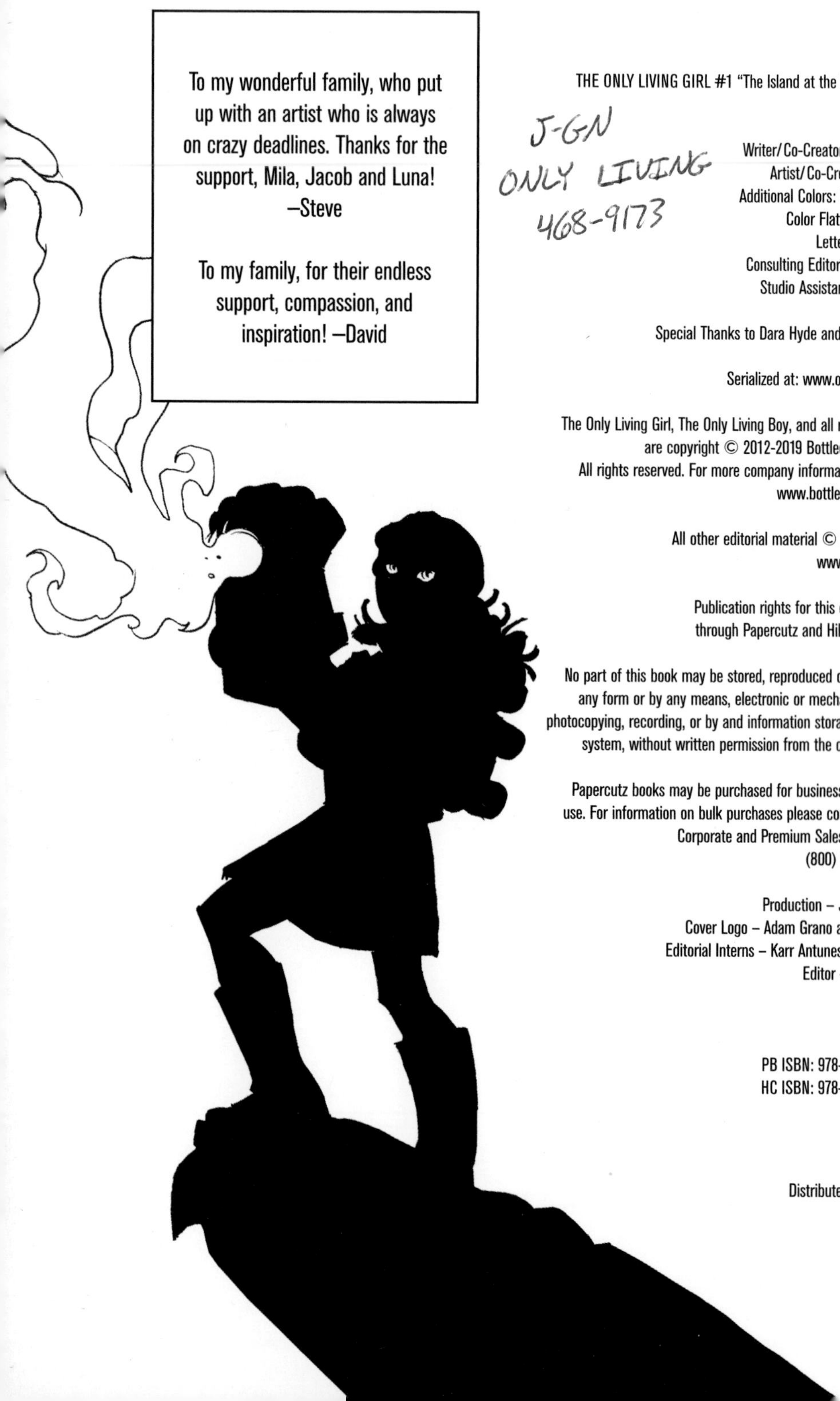

THE ONLY LIVING GIRL #1 "The Island at the Edge of Infinity"

Chapters 1 & 2
Writer/Co-Creator: David Gallaher
Artist/Co-Creator: Steve Ellis
Additional Colors: Chris Sotomayor
Color Flatting: Ryan Leary
Lettering: Nate Pride
Consulting Editor: Janelle Asselin
Studio Assistant: Jen Lightfoot

Special Thanks to Dara Hyde and Vanessa Shealy

Serialized at: www.onlylivinggirl.com

Production – JayJay Jackson
Cover Logo – Adam Grano and Dawn Guzzo
Editorial Interns – Karr Antunes, Spenser Nellis
Editor – Jeff Whitman
Jim Salicrup
Editor-in-Chief

PB ISBN: 978-1-5458-0202-1
HC ISBN: 978-1-5458-0203-8

Printed in India
April 2019

Distributed by Macmillan
First Printing

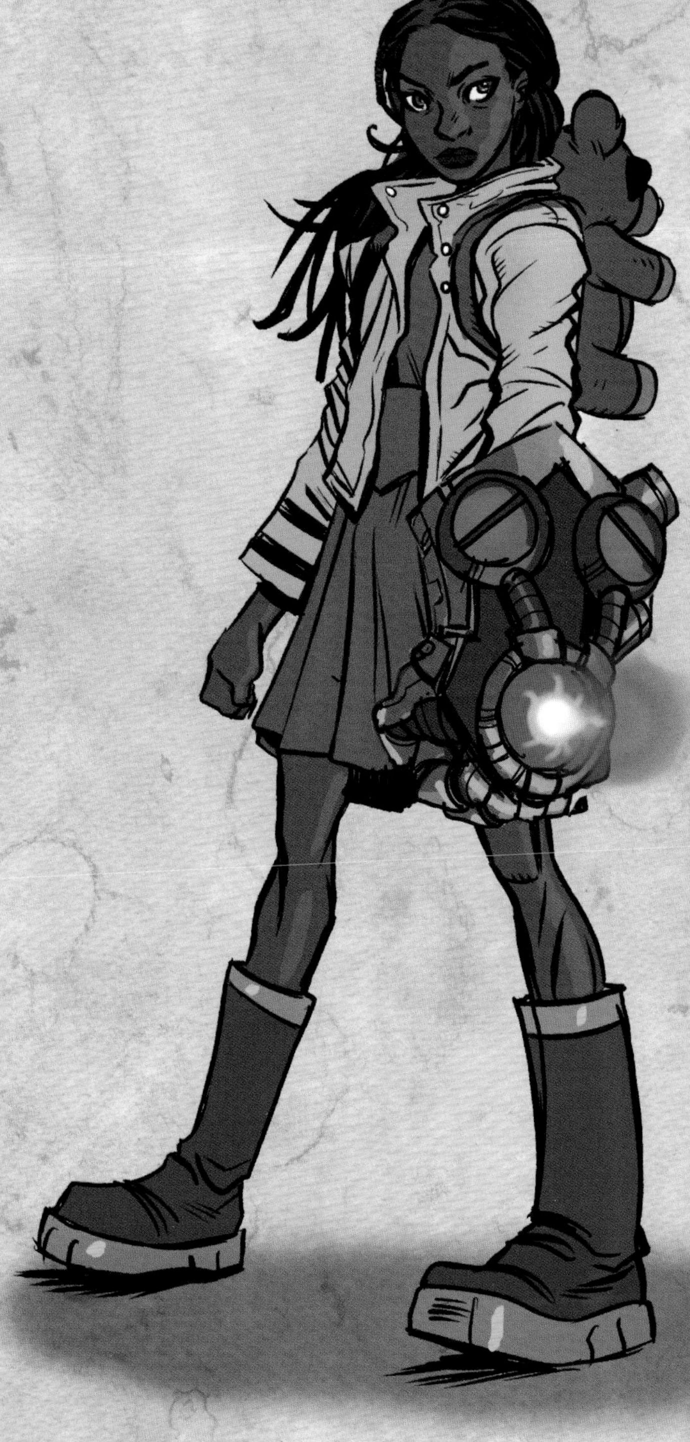

CHAPTER ONE

Previously in...

THE ONLY LIVING BOY

Awake after years of suspended animation, Zandra Parfitt is haunted by memories of her past. Now, as the only living girl left, she must redeem her father's legacy, while trying to survive on a brave new world, where danger and adventure await her.

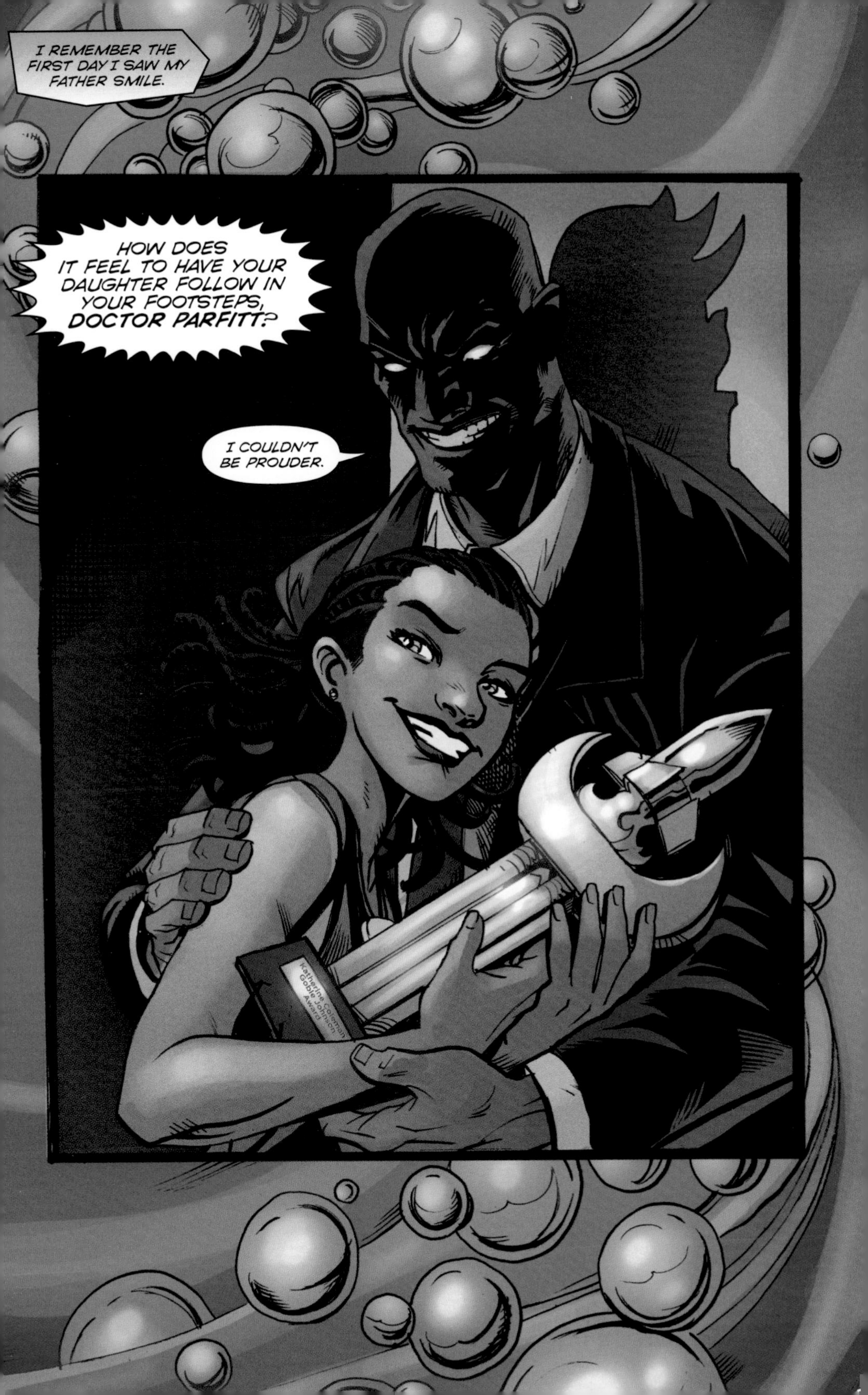
I REMEMBER THE FIRST DAY I SAW MY FATHER SMILE.
HOW DOES IT FEEL TO HAVE YOUR DAUGHTER FOLLOW IN YOUR FOOTSTEPS, DOCTOR PARFITT?
I COULDN'T BE PROUDER.
Katherine Coleman Goble Johnson Award

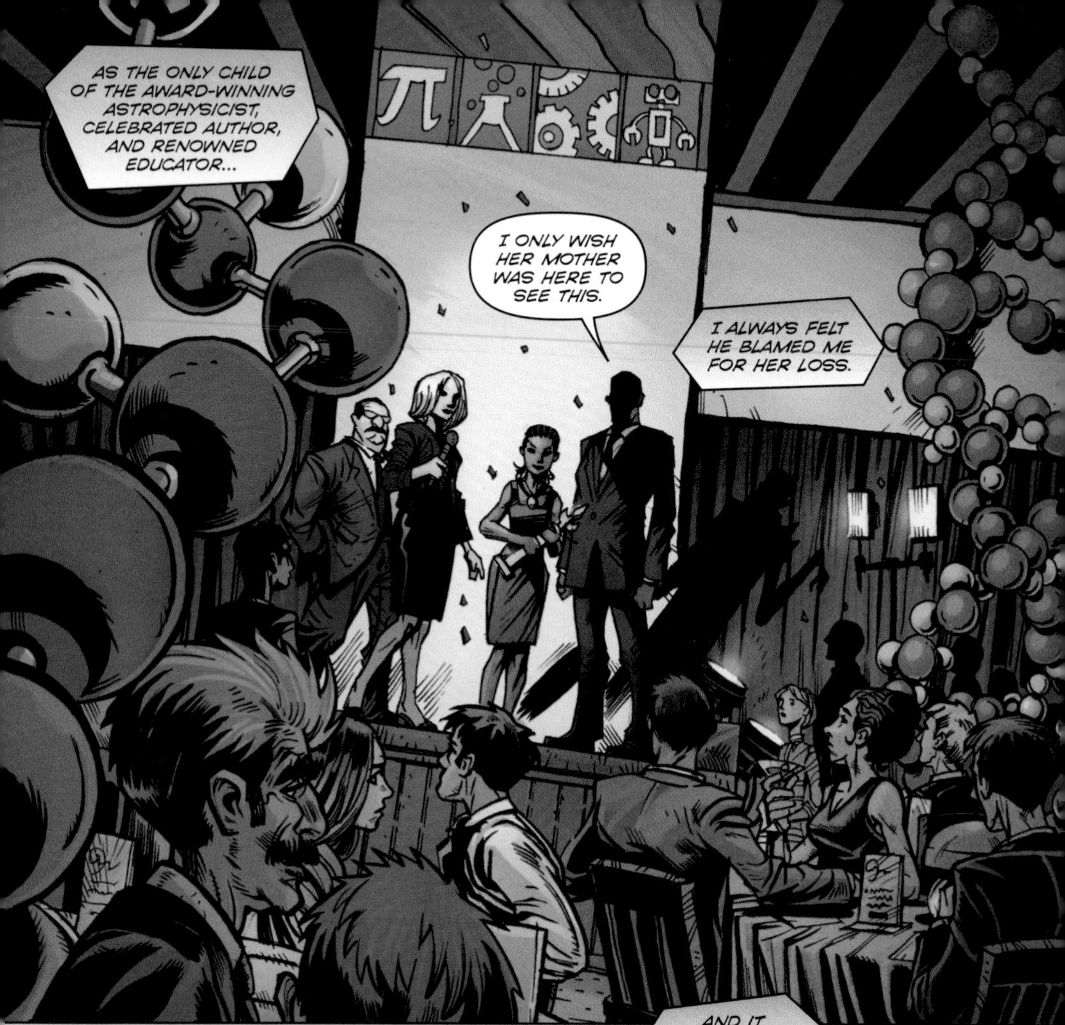
AS THE ONLY CHILD OF THE AWARD-WINNING ASTROPHYSICIST, CELEBRATED AUTHOR, AND RENOWNED EDUCATOR...
I ONLY WISH HER MOTHER WAS HERE TO SEE THIS.
I ALWAYS FELT HE BLAMED ME FOR HER LOSS.

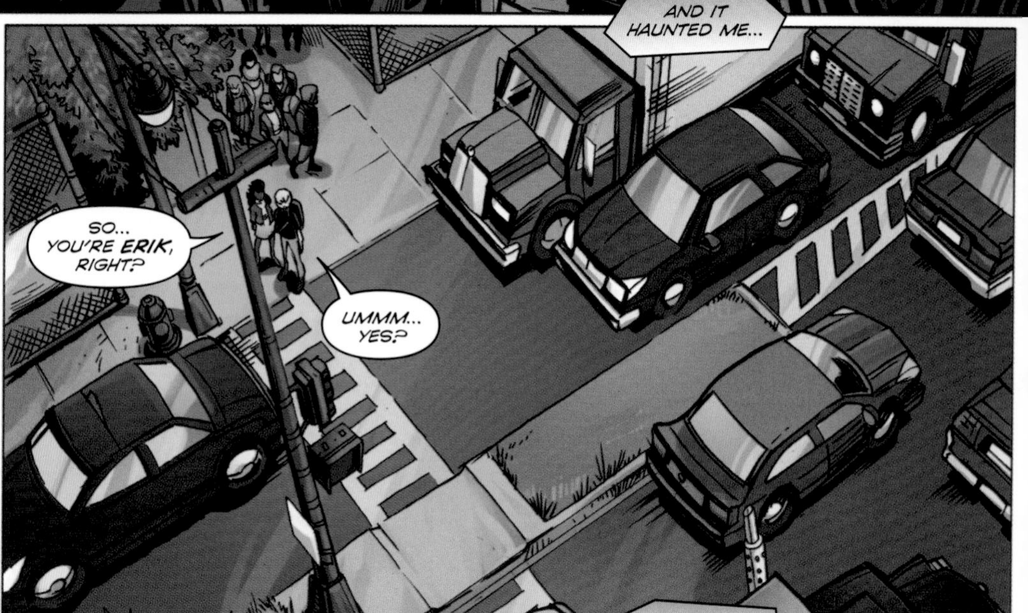
AND IT HAUNTED ME...
SO... YOU'RE ERIK, RIGHT?
UMMM... YES?
...EVERYWHERE I WENT.

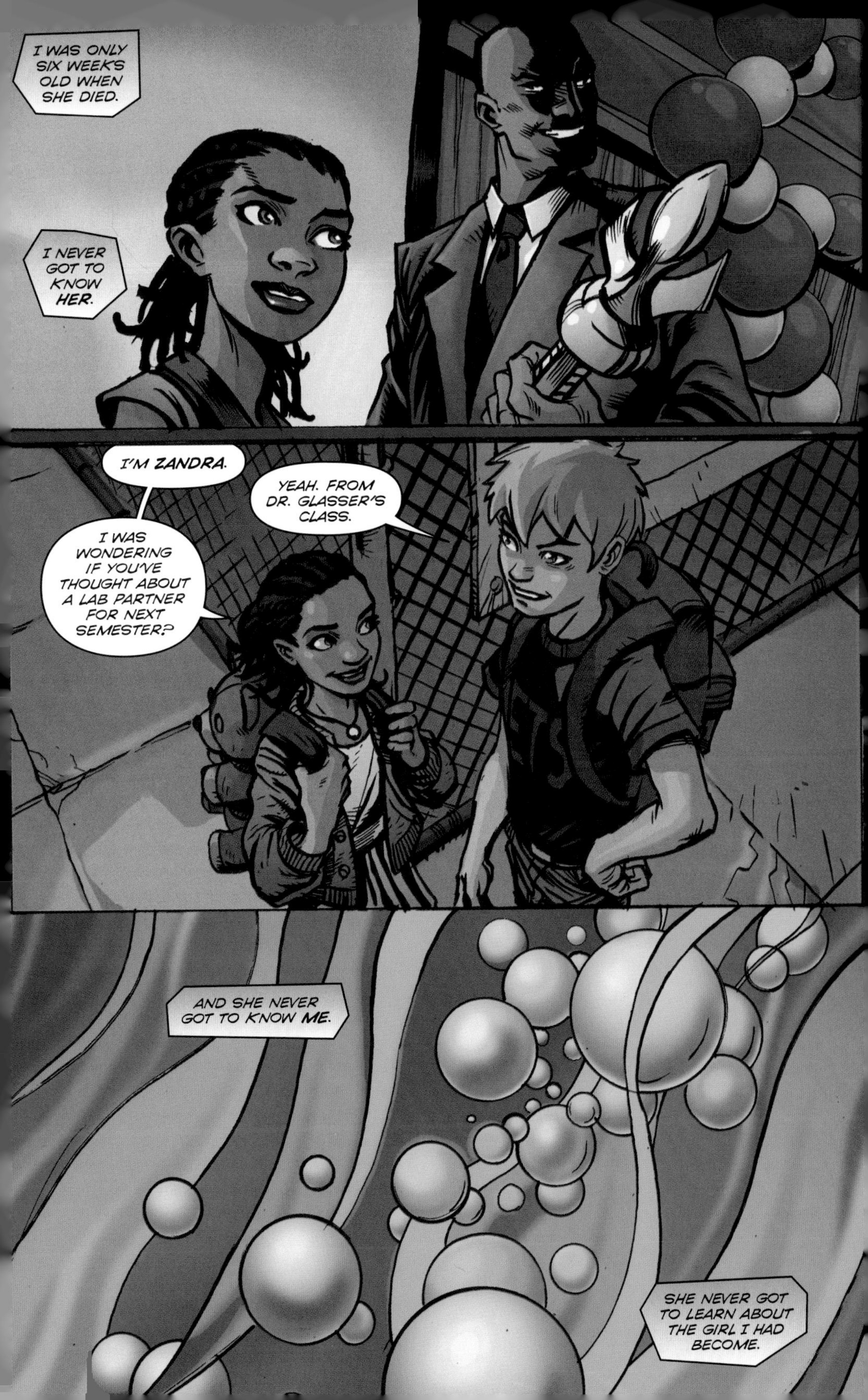
I WAS ONLY SIX WEEKS OLD WHEN SHE DIED.
I NEVER GOT TO KNOW HER.
I'M ZANDRA.
I WAS WONDERING IF YOU'VE THOUGHT ABOUT A LAB PARTNER FOR NEXT SEMESTER?
YEAH. FROM DR. GLASSER'S CLASS.
AND SHE NEVER GOT TO KNOW ME.
SHE NEVER GOT TO LEARN ABOUT THE GIRL I HAD BECOME.

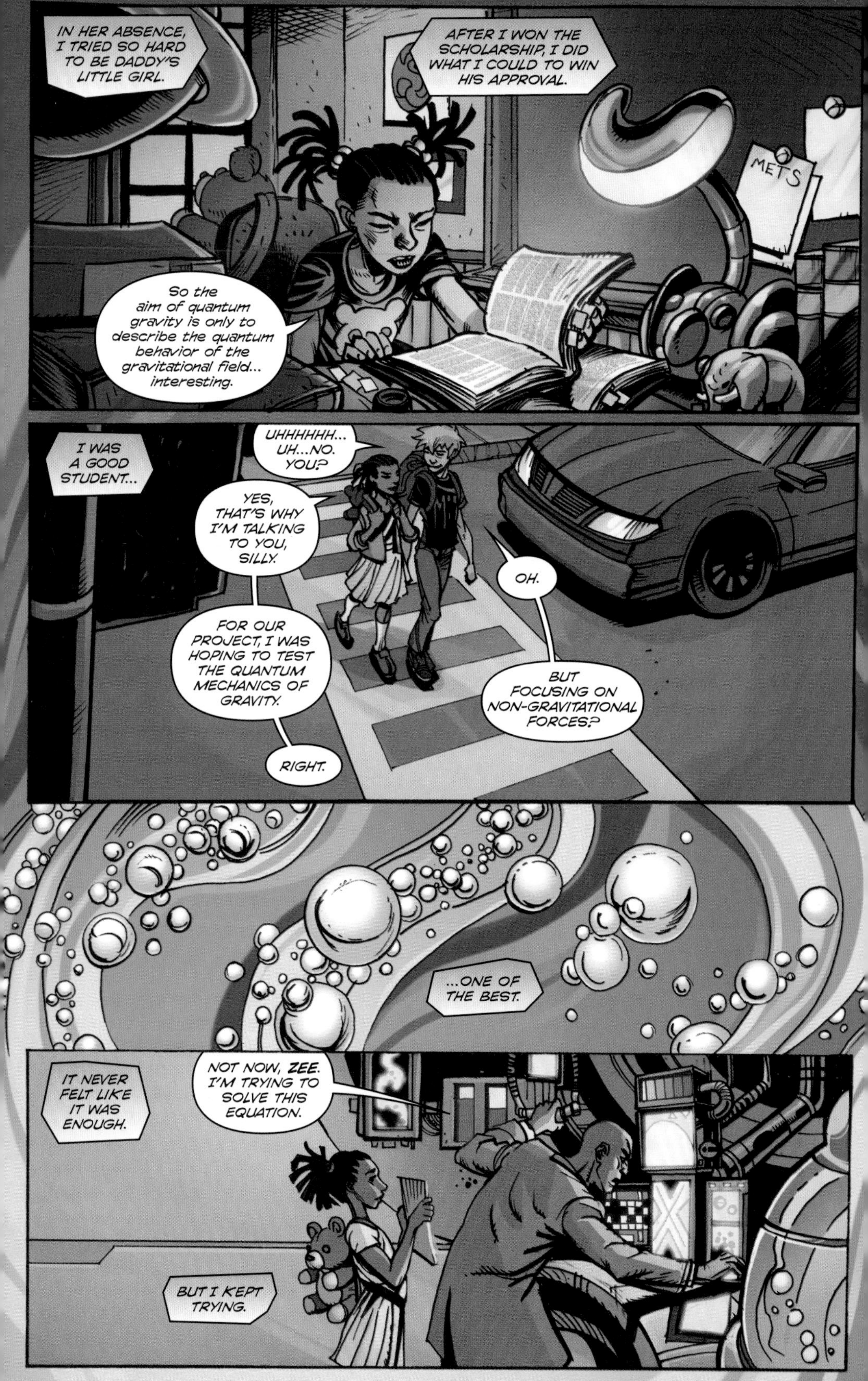
IN HER ABSENCE, I TRIED SO HARD TO BE DADDY'S LITTLE GIRL.
AFTER I WON THE SCHOLARSHIP, I DID WHAT I COULD TO WIN HIS APPROVAL.
METS
So the aim of quantum gravity is only to describe the quantum behavior of the gravitational field... interesting.
I WAS A GOOD STUDENT...
UHHHHHH... UH...NO. YOU?
YES, THAT'S WHY I'M TALKING TO YOU, SILLY.
OH.
FOR OUR PROJECT, I WAS HOPING TO TEST THE QUANTUM MECHANICS OF GRAVITY.
BUT FOCUSING ON NON-GRAVITATIONAL FORCES?
RIGHT.
...ONE OF THE BEST.
IT NEVER FELT LIKE IT WAS ENOUGH.
NOT NOW, ZEE. I'M TRYING TO SOLVE THIS EQUATION.
BUT I KEPT TRYING.

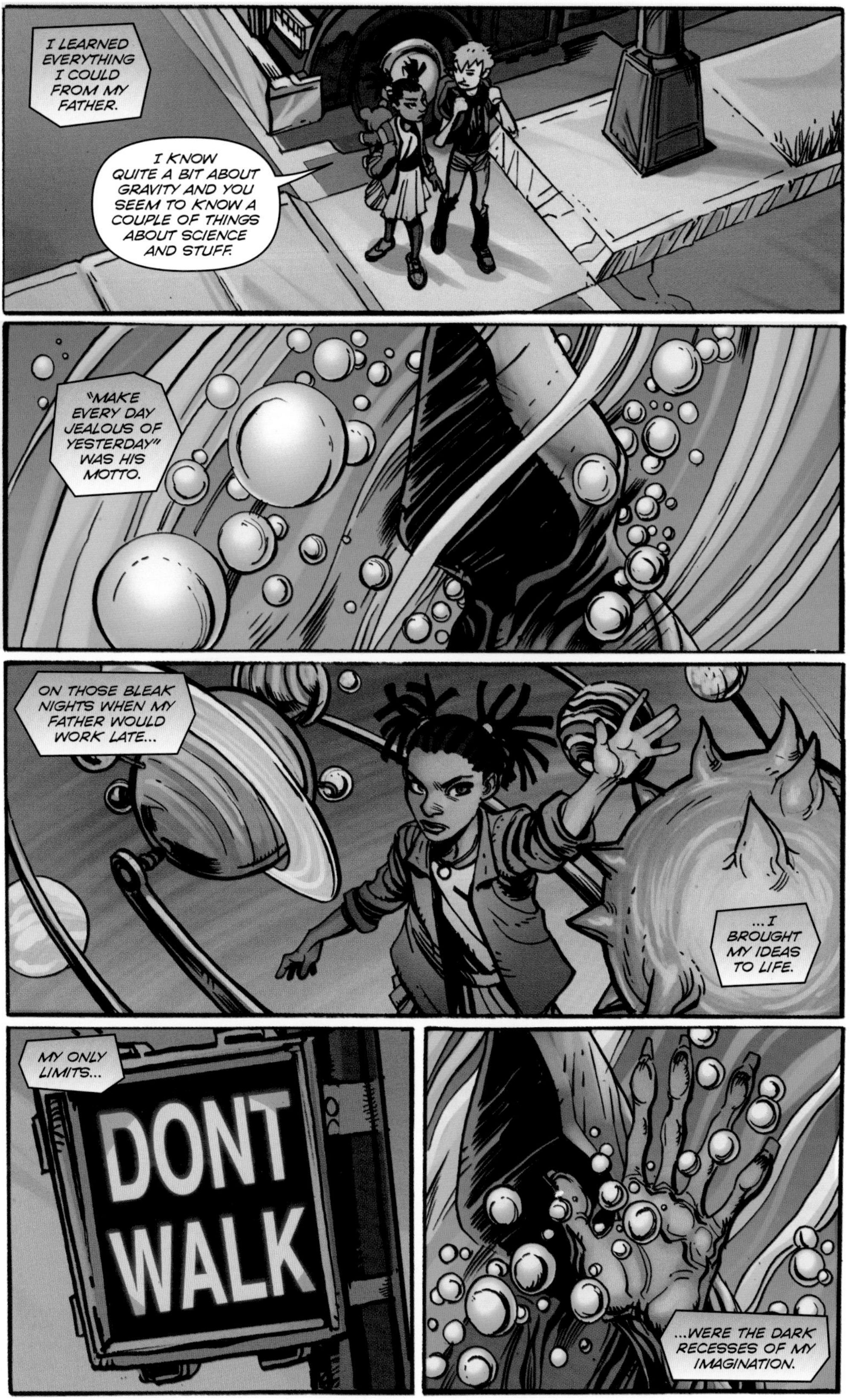
I LEARNED EVERYTHING I COULD FROM MY FATHER.
I KNOW QUITE A BIT ABOUT GRAVITY AND YOU SEEM TO KNOW A COUPLE OF THINGS ABOUT SCIENCE AND STUFF.
"MAKE EVERY DAY JEALOUS OF YESTERDAY" WAS HIS MOTTO.
ON THOSE BLEAK NIGHTS WHEN MY FATHER WOULD WORK LATE...
...I BROUGHT MY IDEAS TO LIFE.
MY ONLY LIMITS...
DONT WALK
...WERE THE DARK RECESSES OF MY IMAGINATION.

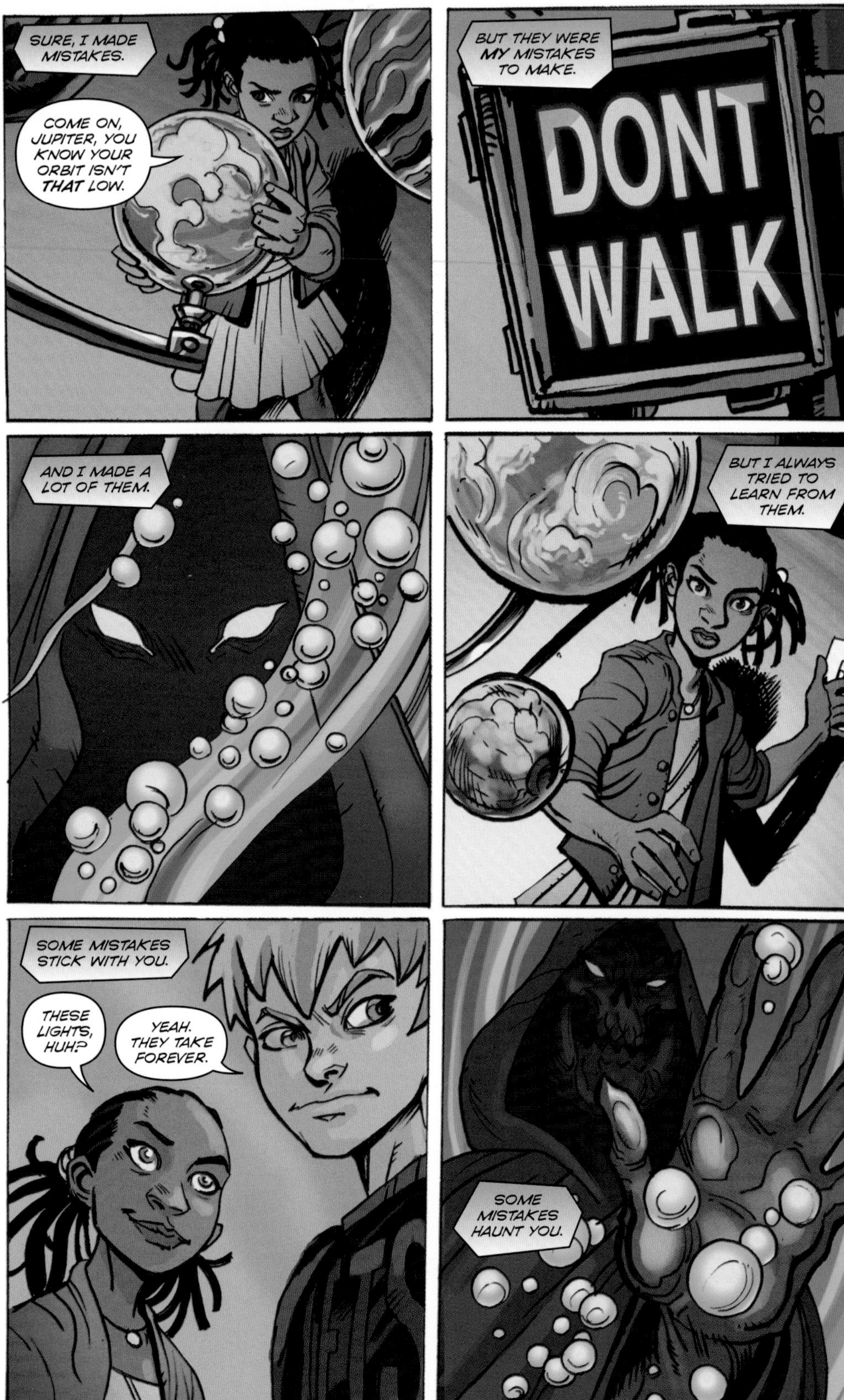
SURE, I MADE MISTAKES.
COME ON, JUPITER, YOU KNOW YOUR ORBIT ISN'T THAT LOW.
BUT THEY WERE MY MISTAKES TO MAKE.
DONT WALK
AND I MADE A LOT OF THEM.
BUT I ALWAYS TRIED TO LEARN FROM THEM.
SOME MISTAKES STICK WITH YOU.
THESE LIGHTS, HUH?
YEAH. THEY TAKE FOREVER.
SOME MISTAKES HAUNT YOU.

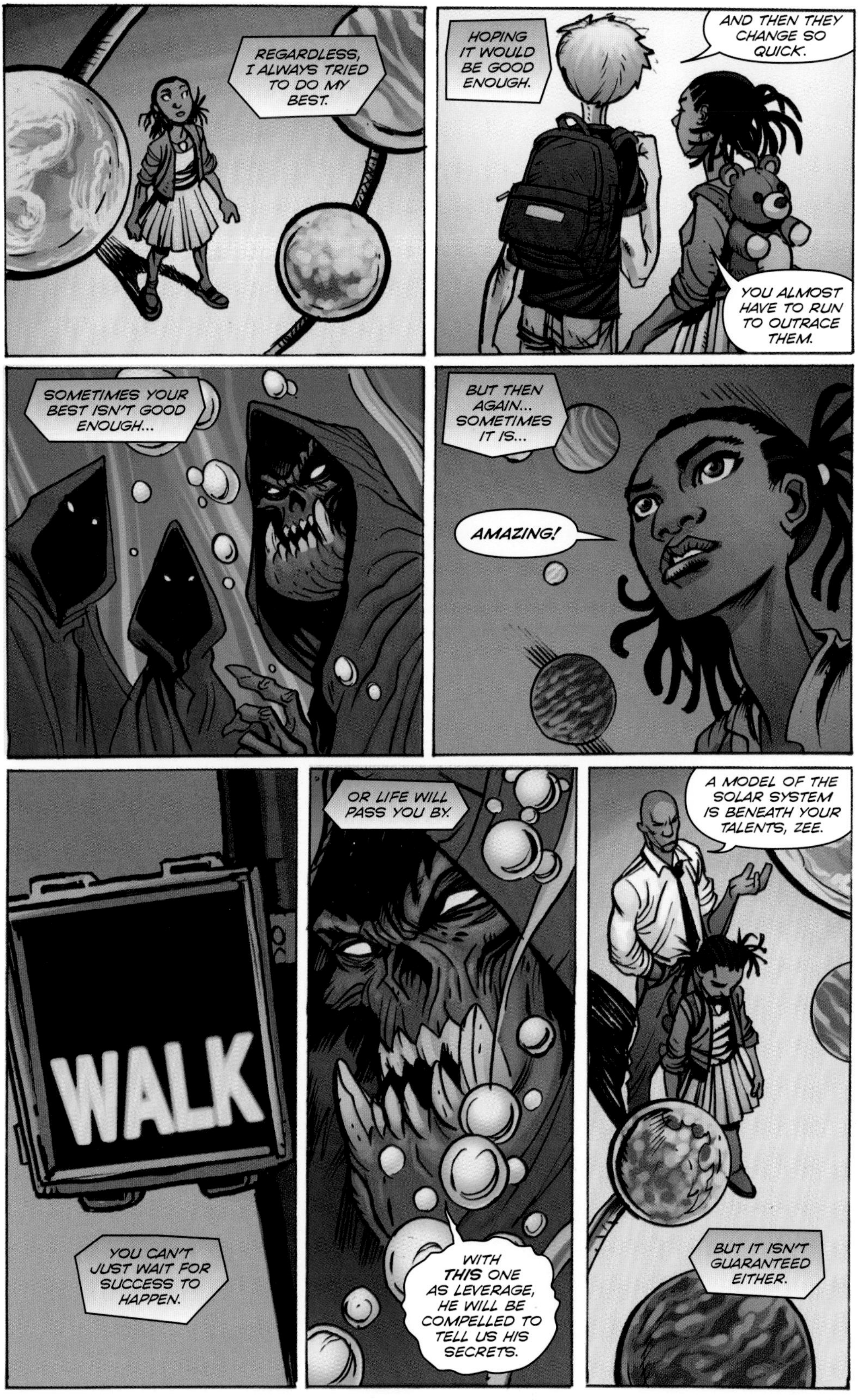
REGARDLESS, I ALWAYS TRIED TO DO MY BEST.
HOPING IT WOULD BE GOOD ENOUGH.
AND THEN THEY CHANGE SO QUICK.
YOU ALMOST HAVE TO RUN TO OUTRACE THEM.
SOMETIMES YOUR BEST ISN'T GOOD ENOUGH...
BUT THEN AGAIN... SOMETIMES IT IS...
AMAZING!
WALK
YOU CAN'T JUST WAIT FOR SUCCESS TO HAPPEN.
OR LIFE WILL PASS YOU BY.
WITH THIS ONE AS LEVERAGE, HE WILL BE COMPELLED TO TELL US HIS SECRETS.
A MODEL OF THE SOLAR SYSTEM IS BENEATH YOUR TALENTS, ZEE.
BUT IT ISN'T GUARANTEED EITHER.

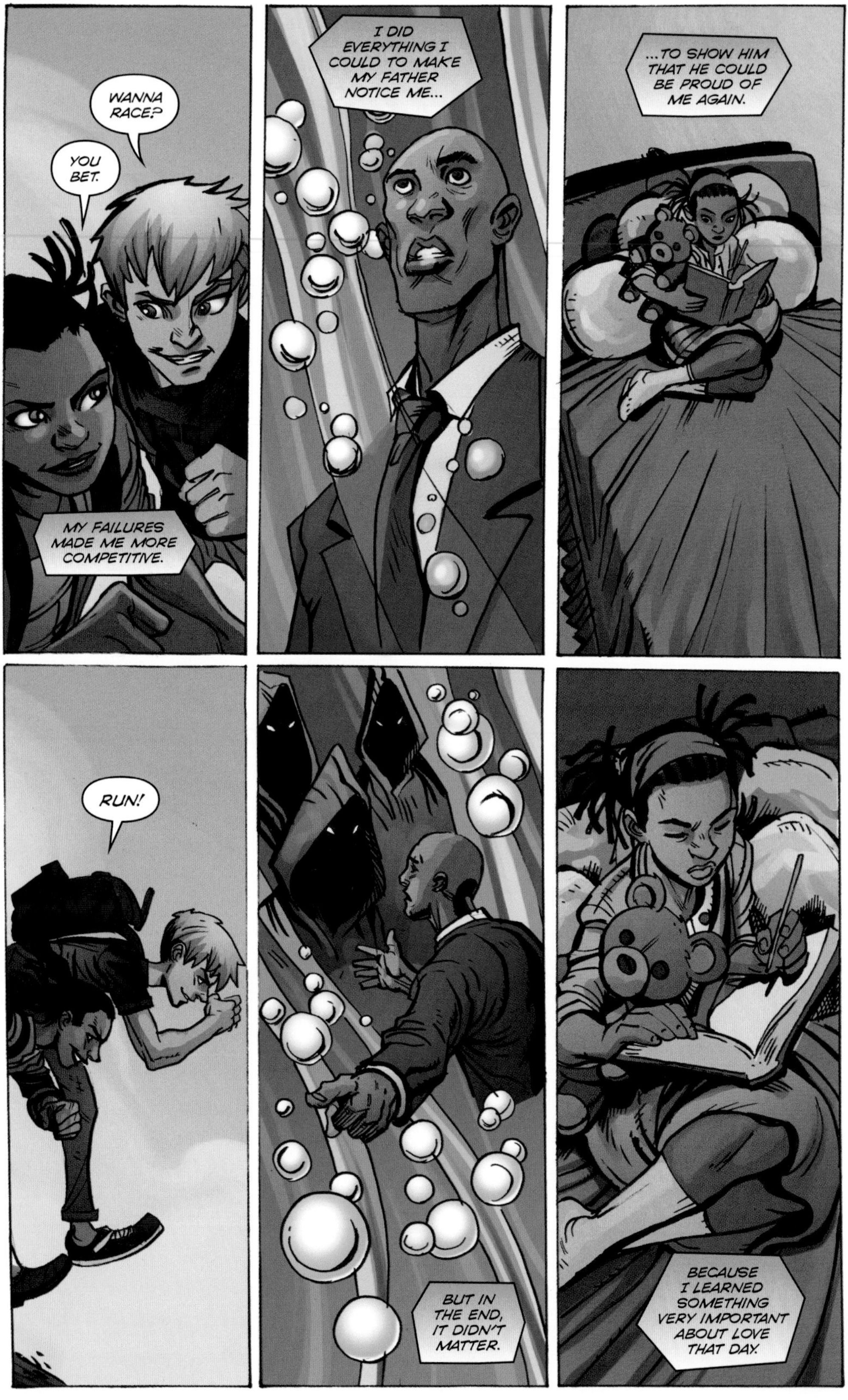
WANNA RACE?
YOU BET.
MY FAILURES MADE ME MORE COMPETITIVE.
I DID EVERYTHING I COULD TO MAKE MY FATHER NOTICE ME...
...TO SHOW HIM THAT HE COULD BE PROUD OF ME AGAIN.
RUN!
BUT IN THE END, IT DIDN'T MATTER.
BECAUSE I LEARNED SOMETHING VERY IMPORTANT ABOUT LOVE THAT DAY.

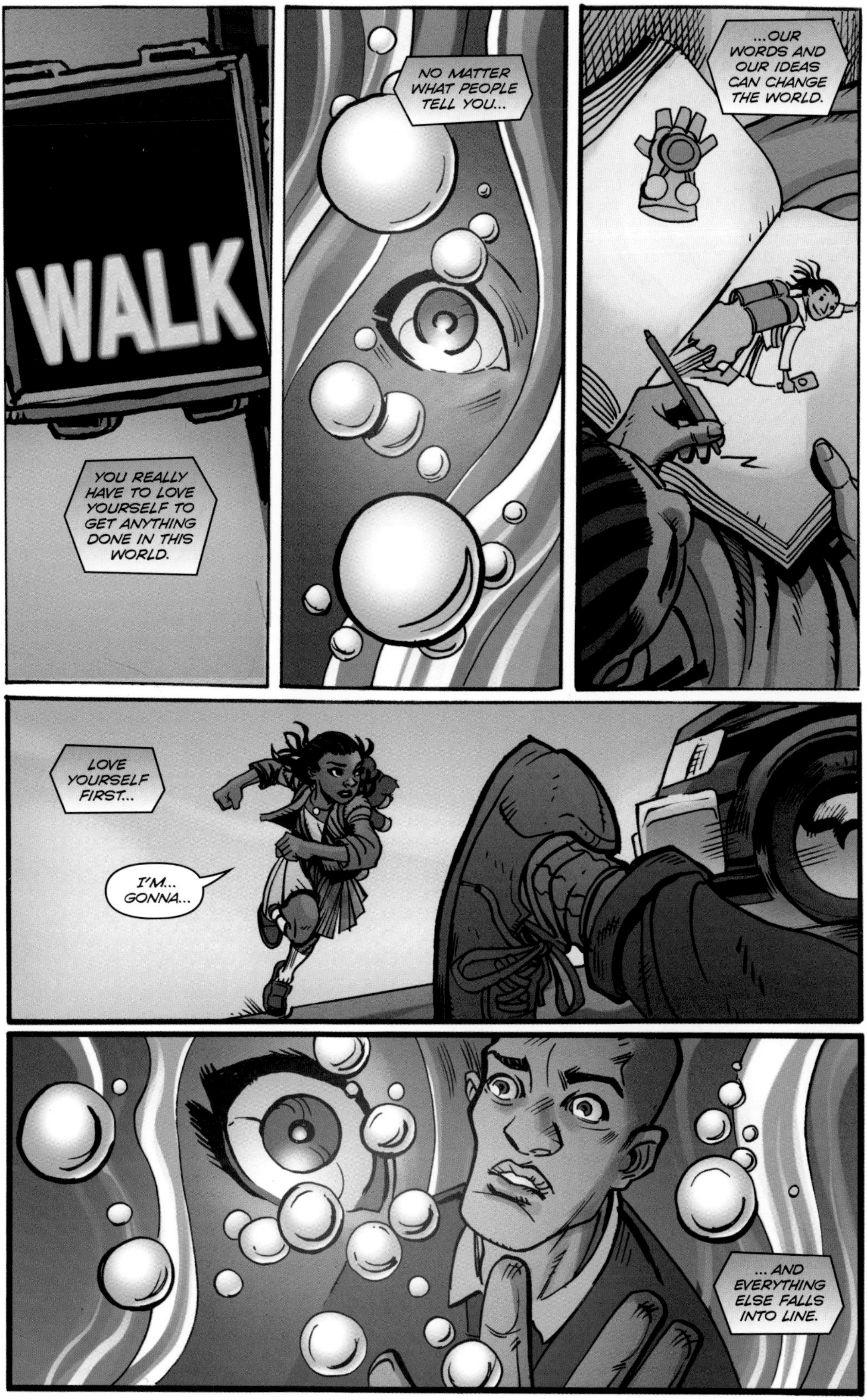
WALK
YOU REALLY HAVE TO LOVE YOURSELF TO GET ANYTHING DONE IN THIS WORLD.
NO MATTER WHAT PEOPLE TELL YOU...
...OUR WORDS AND OUR IDEAS CAN CHANGE THE WORLD.
LOVE YOURSELF FIRST...
I'M... GONNA...
... AND EVERYTHING ELSE FALLS INTO LINE.

THAT WAS THE MOMENT...

THE MOMENT I SOLVED THE PROBLEM OF BEING A KID.

I MISS THAT MOMENT.

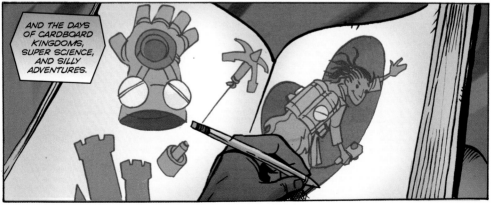

AND THE DAYS OF CARDBOARD KINGDOMS, SUPER SCIENCE, AND SILLY ADVENTURES.

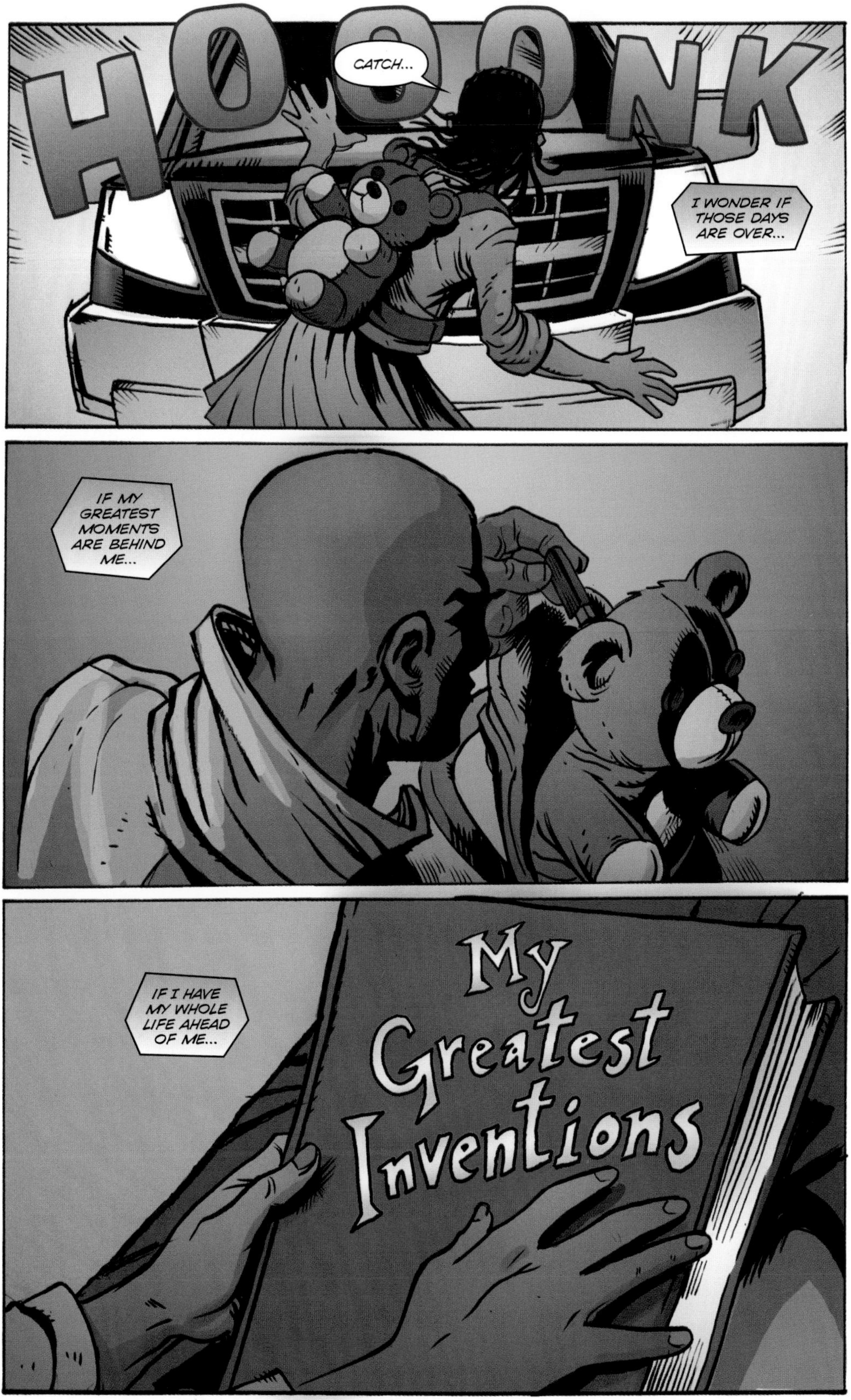
HOOONK
CATCH...
I WONDER IF THOSE DAYS ARE OVER...
IF MY GREATEST MOMENTS ARE BEHIND ME...
IF I HAVE MY WHOLE LIFE AHEAD OF ME...
My Greatest Inventions

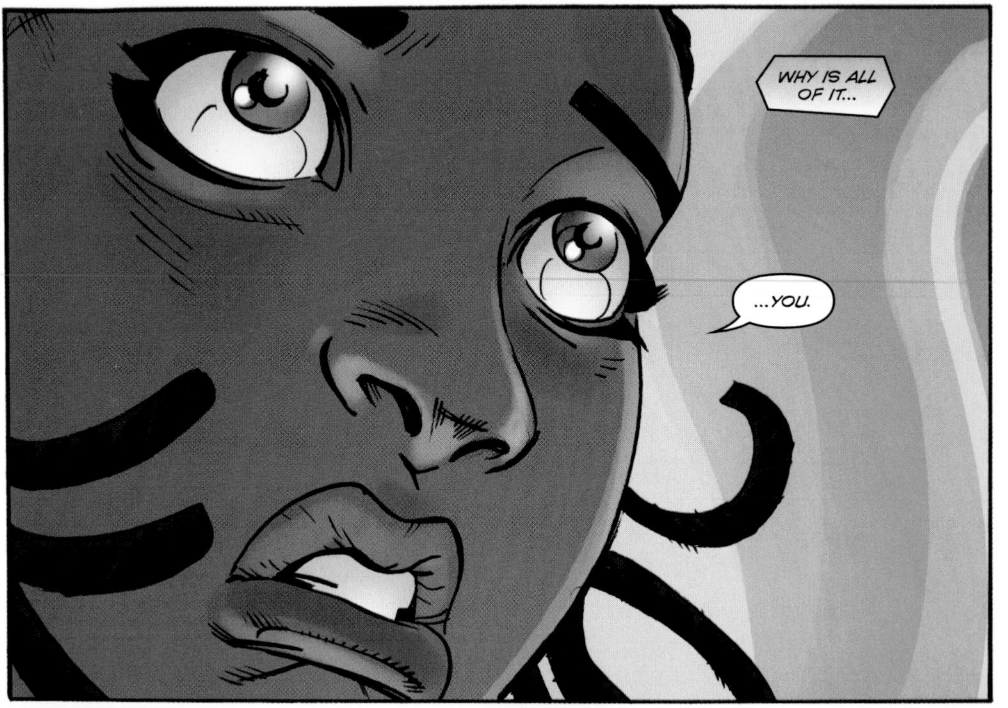
WHY IS ALL OF IT...
...YOU.

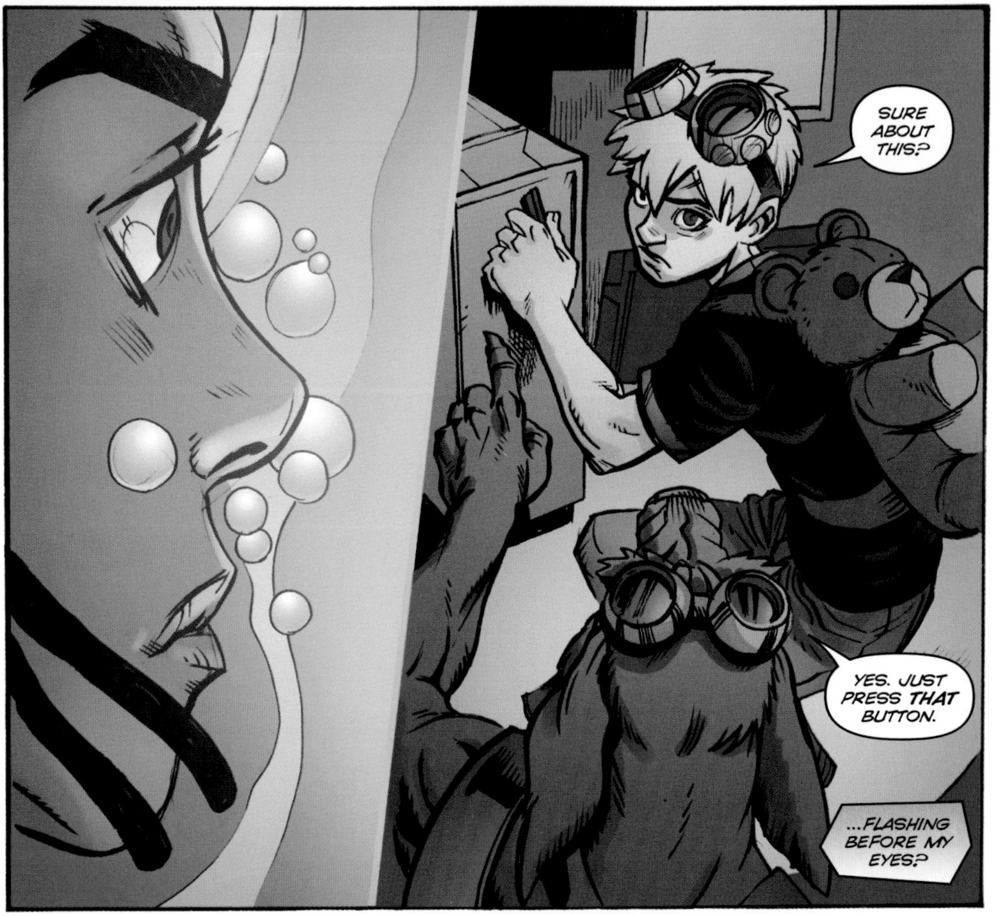
SURE ABOUT THIS?
YES. JUST PRESS THAT BUTTON.
...FLASHING BEFORE MY EYES?

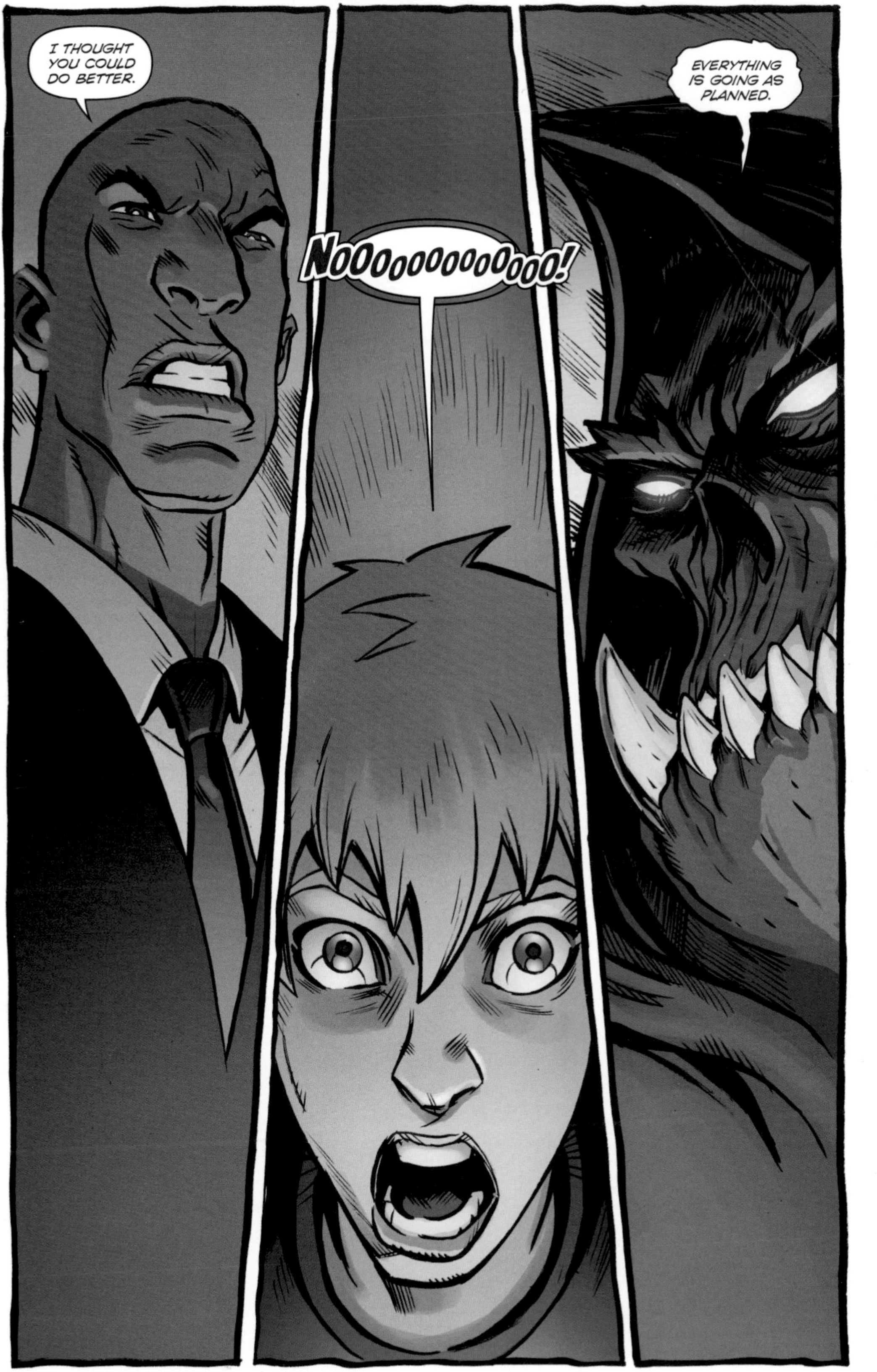
I THOUGHT YOU COULD DO BETTER.
NOOOOOOOOOOOOO!
EVERYTHING IS GOING AS PLANNED.

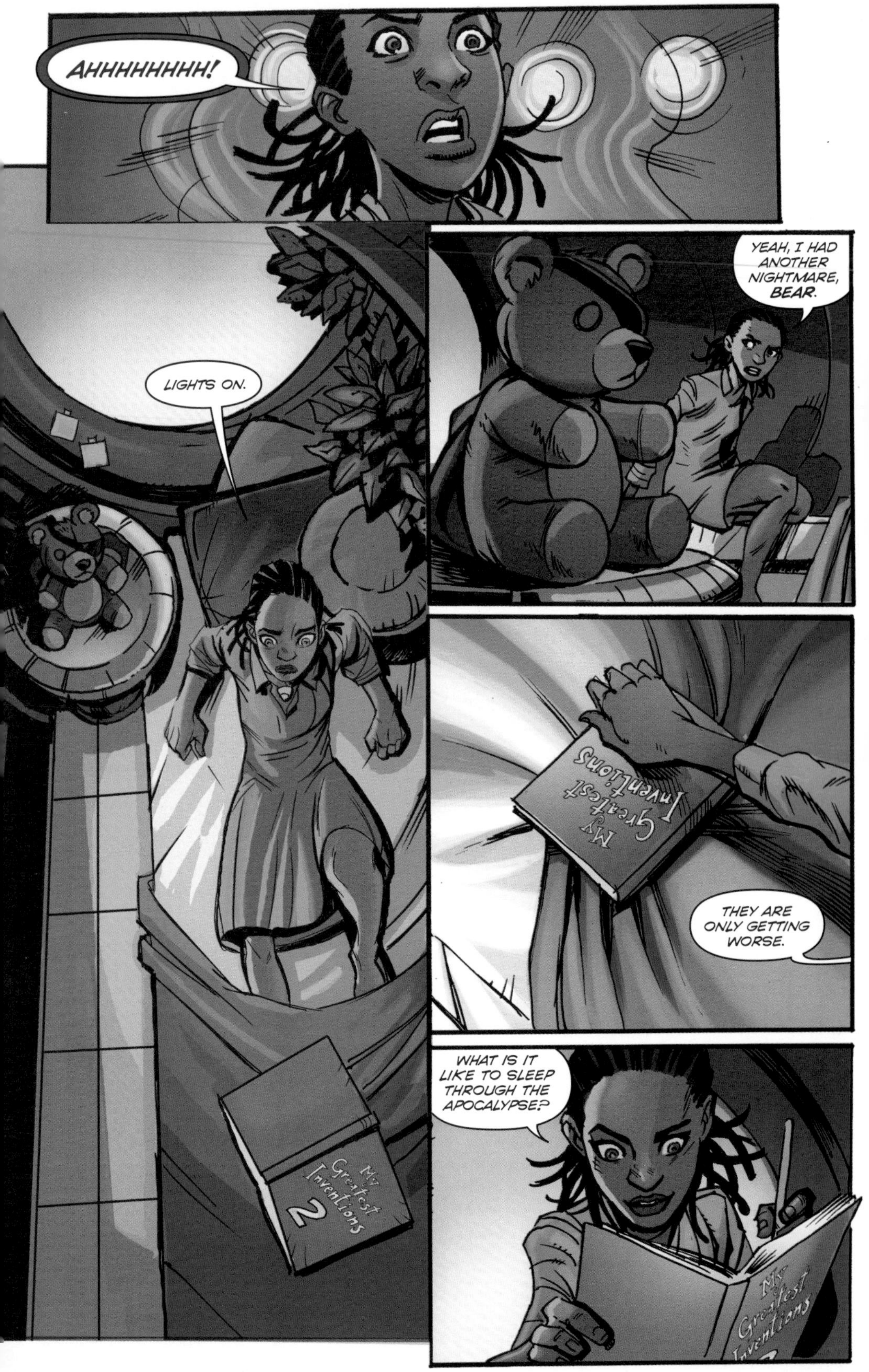
AHHHHHHHH!
LIGHTS ON.
YEAH, I HAD ANOTHER NIGHTMARE, BEAR.
My Greatest Inventions 2
My Greatest Inventions
THEY ARE ONLY GETTING WORSE.
WHAT IS IT LIKE TO SLEEP THROUGH THE APOCALYPSE?
My Greatest Inventions

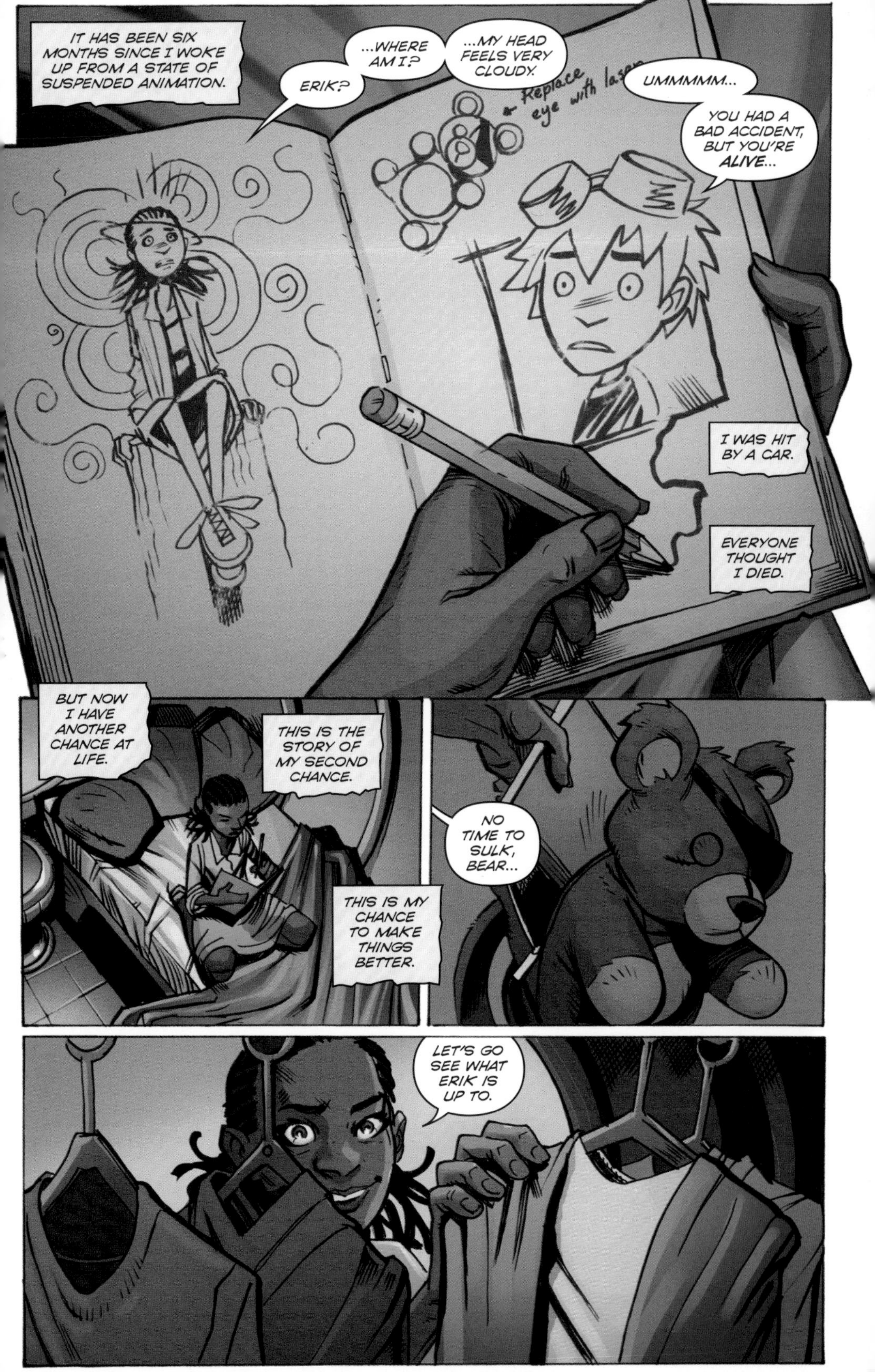
IT HAS BEEN SIX MONTHS SINCE I WOKE UP FROM A STATE OF SUSPENDED ANIMATION.
ERIK?
...WHERE AM I?
...MY HEAD FEELS VERY CLOUDY.
UMMMMM...
YOU HAD A BAD ACCIDENT, BUT YOU'RE ALIVE...
Replace eye with laser
I WAS HIT BY A CAR.
EVERYONE THOUGHT I DIED.
BUT NOW I HAVE ANOTHER CHANCE AT LIFE.
THIS IS THE STORY OF MY SECOND CHANCE.
THIS IS MY CHANCE TO MAKE THINGS BETTER.
NO TIME TO SULK, BEAR...
LET'S GO SEE WHAT ERIK IS UP TO.

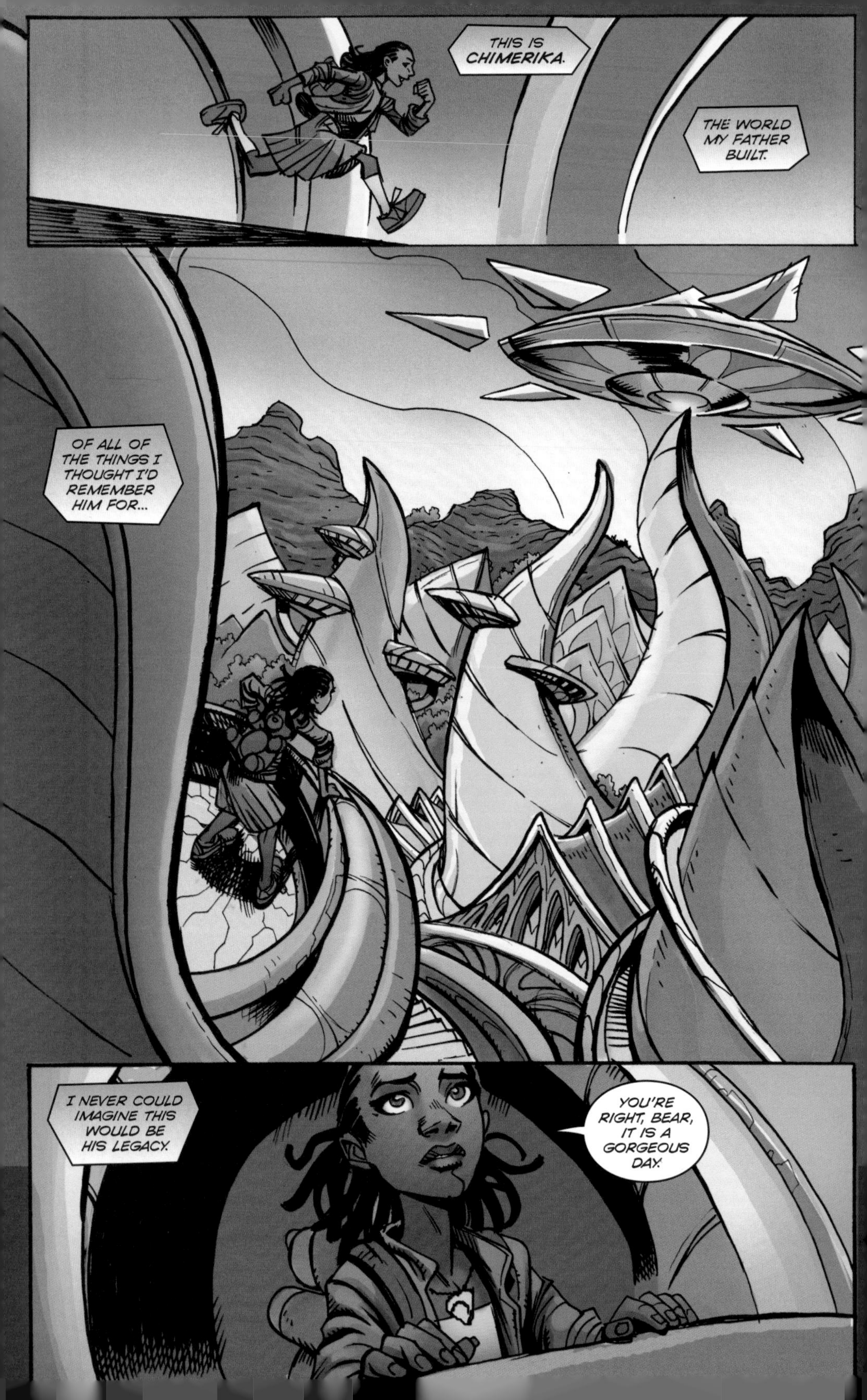
THIS IS CHIMERIKA.
THE WORLD MY FATHER BUILT.
OF ALL OF THE THINGS I THOUGHT I'D REMEMBER HIM FOR...
I NEVER COULD IMAGINE THIS WOULD BE HIS LEGACY.
YOU'RE RIGHT, BEAR, IT IS A GORGEOUS DAY.

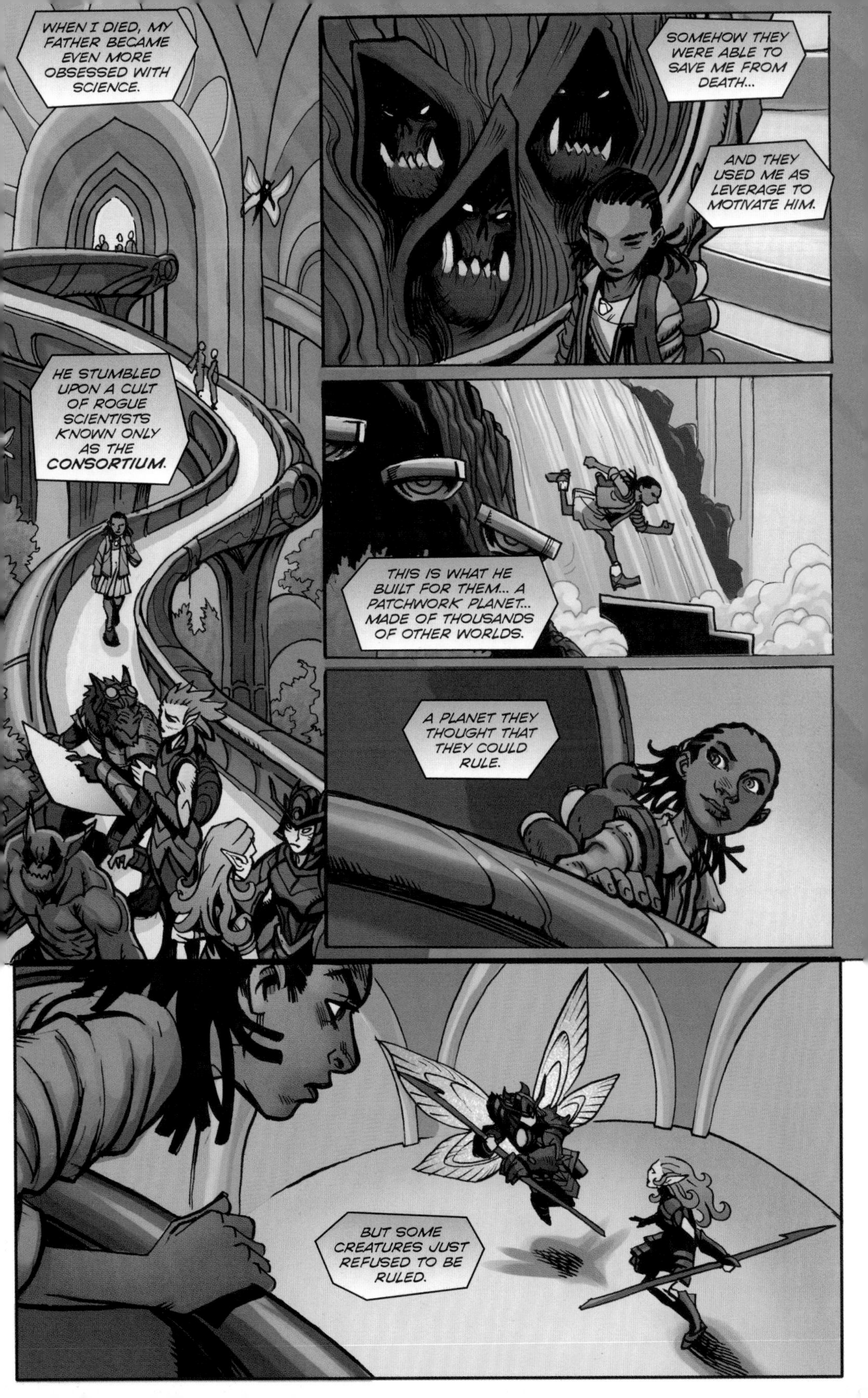
WHEN I DIED, MY FATHER BECAME EVEN MORE OBSESSED WITH SCIENCE.
HE STUMBLED UPON A CULT OF ROGUE SCIENTISTS KNOWN ONLY AS THE **CONSORTIUM**.
SOMEHOW THEY WERE ABLE TO SAVE ME FROM DEATH...
AND THEY USED ME AS LEVERAGE TO MOTIVATE HIM.
THIS IS WHAT HE BUILT FOR THEM... A PATCHWORK PLANET... MADE OF THOUSANDS OF OTHER WORLDS.
A PLANET THEY THOUGHT THAT THEY COULD RULE.
BUT SOME CREATURES JUST REFUSED TO BE RULED.

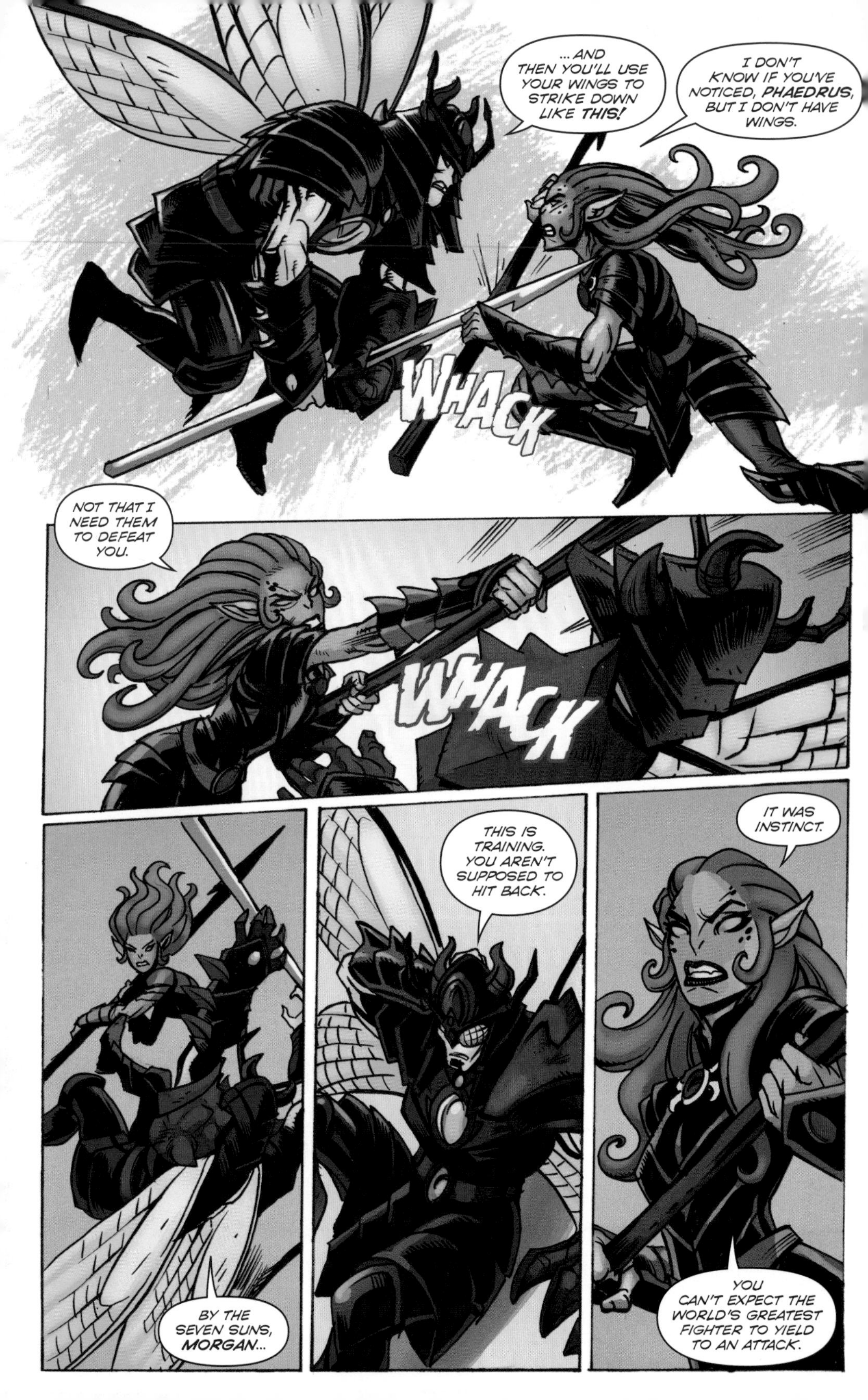
...AND THEN YOU'LL USE YOUR WINGS TO STRIKE DOWN LIKE THIS!
I DON'T KNOW IF YOU'VE NOTICED, PHAEDRUS, BUT I DON'T HAVE WINGS.
WHACK
NOT THAT I NEED THEM TO DEFEAT YOU.
WHACK
BY THE SEVEN SUNS, MORGAN...
THIS IS TRAINING. YOU AREN'T SUPPOSED TO HIT BACK.
IT WAS INSTINCT.
YOU CAN'T EXPECT THE WORLD'S GREATEST FIGHTER TO YIELD TO AN ATTACK.

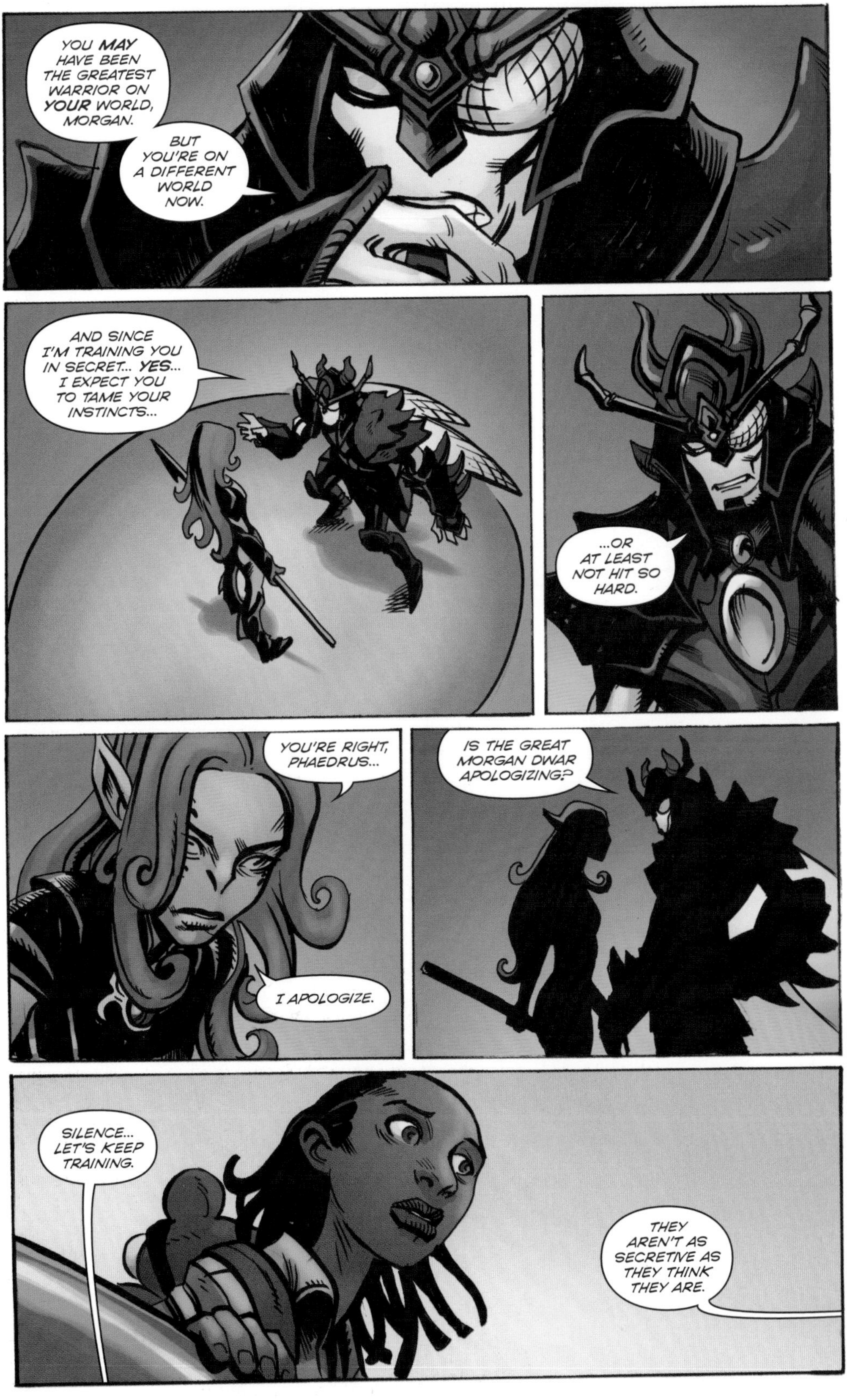
YOU MAY HAVE BEEN THE GREATEST WARRIOR ON YOUR WORLD, MORGAN.
BUT YOU'RE ON A DIFFERENT WORLD NOW.
AND SINCE I'M TRAINING YOU IN SECRET... YES... I EXPECT YOU TO TAME YOUR INSTINCTS...
...OR AT LEAST NOT HIT SO HARD.
YOU'RE RIGHT, PHAEDRUS...
I APOLOGIZE.
IS THE GREAT MORGAN DWAR APOLOGIZING?
SILENCE... LET'S KEEP TRAINING.
THEY AREN'T AS SECRETIVE AS THEY THINK THEY ARE.

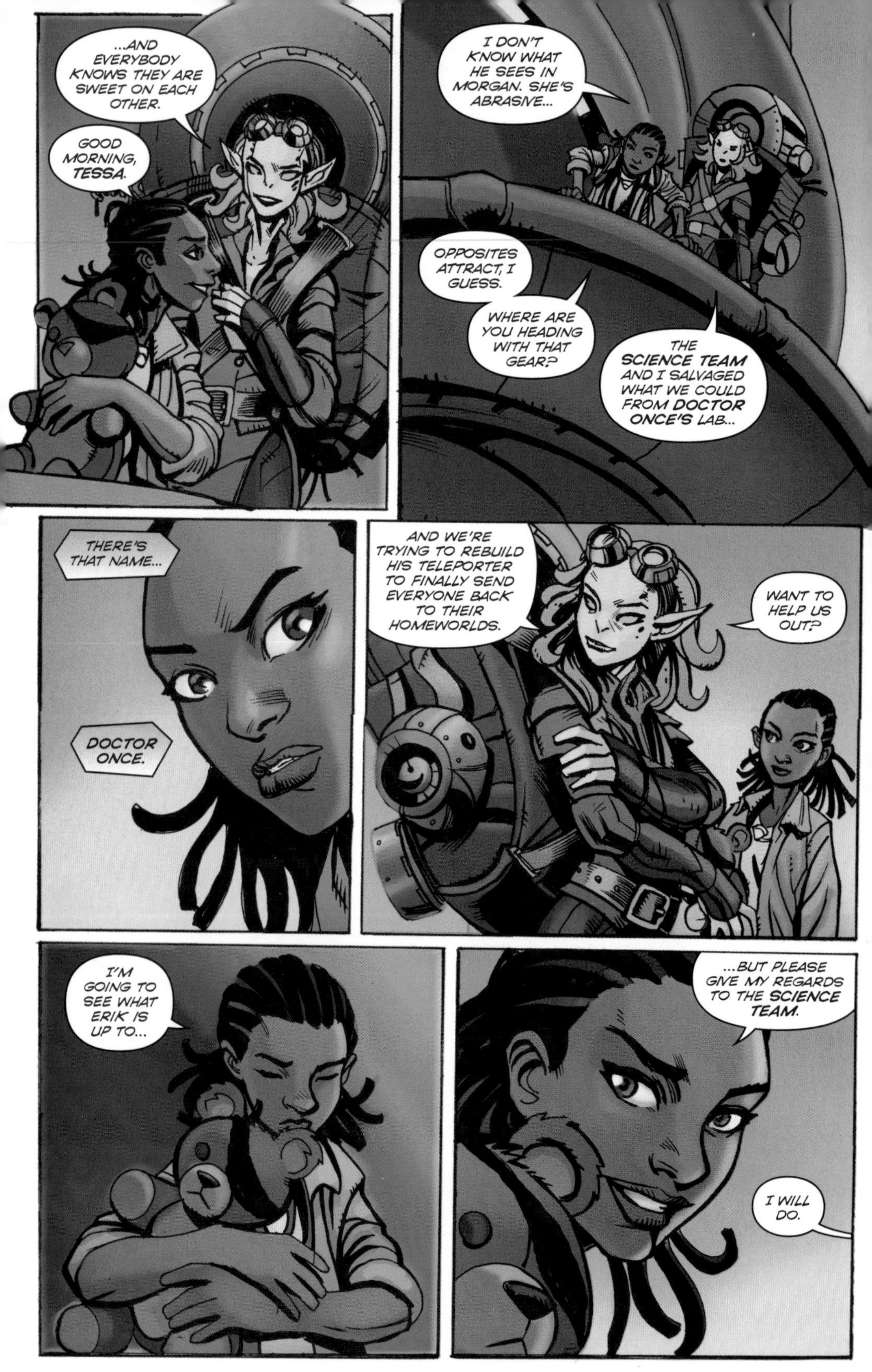
...AND EVERYBODY KNOWS THEY ARE SWEET ON EACH OTHER.
GOOD MORNING, TESSA.
I DON'T KNOW WHAT HE SEES IN MORGAN. SHE'S ABRASIVE...
OPPOSITES ATTRACT, I GUESS.
WHERE ARE YOU HEADING WITH THAT GEAR?
THE SCIENCE TEAM AND I SALVAGED WHAT WE COULD FROM DOCTOR ONCE'S LAB...
THERE'S THAT NAME...
DOCTOR ONCE.
AND WE'RE TRYING TO REBUILD HIS TELEPORTER TO FINALLY SEND EVERYONE BACK TO THEIR HOMEWORLDS.
WANT TO HELP US OUT?
I'M GOING TO SEE WHAT ERIK IS UP TO...
...BUT PLEASE GIVE MY REGARDS TO THE SCIENCE TEAM.
I WILL DO.

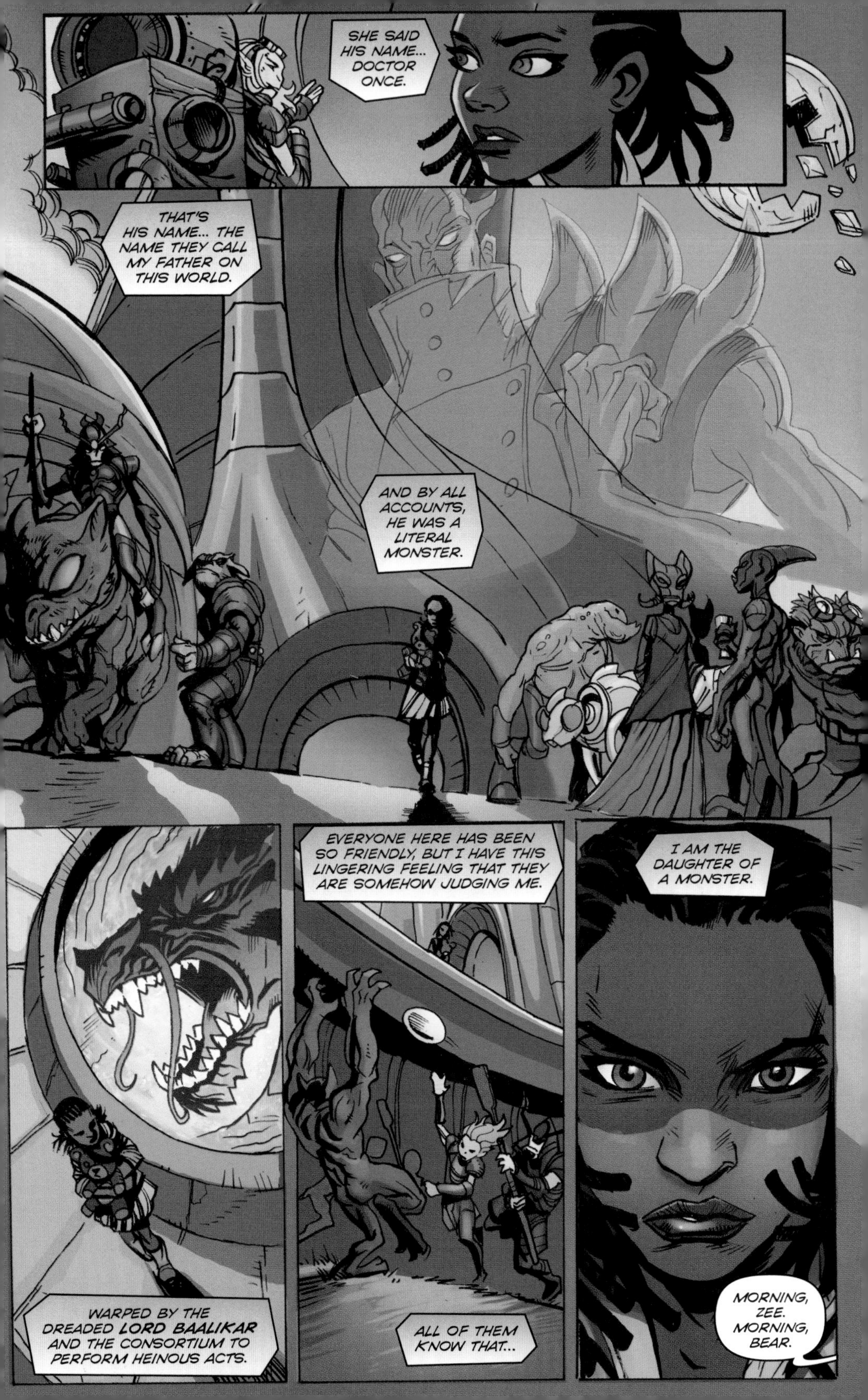
SHE SAID HIS NAME... DOCTOR ONCE.
THAT'S HIS NAME... THE NAME THEY CALL MY FATHER ON THIS WORLD.
AND BY ALL ACCOUNTS, HE WAS A LITERAL MONSTER.
WARPED BY THE DREADED LORD BAALIKAR AND THE CONSORTIUM TO PERFORM HEINOUS ACTS.
EVERYONE HERE HAS BEEN SO FRIENDLY, BUT I HAVE THIS LINGERING FEELING THAT THEY ARE SOMEHOW JUDGING ME.
ALL OF THEM KNOW THAT...
I AM THE DAUGHTER OF A MONSTER.
MORNING, ZEE. MORNING, BEAR.

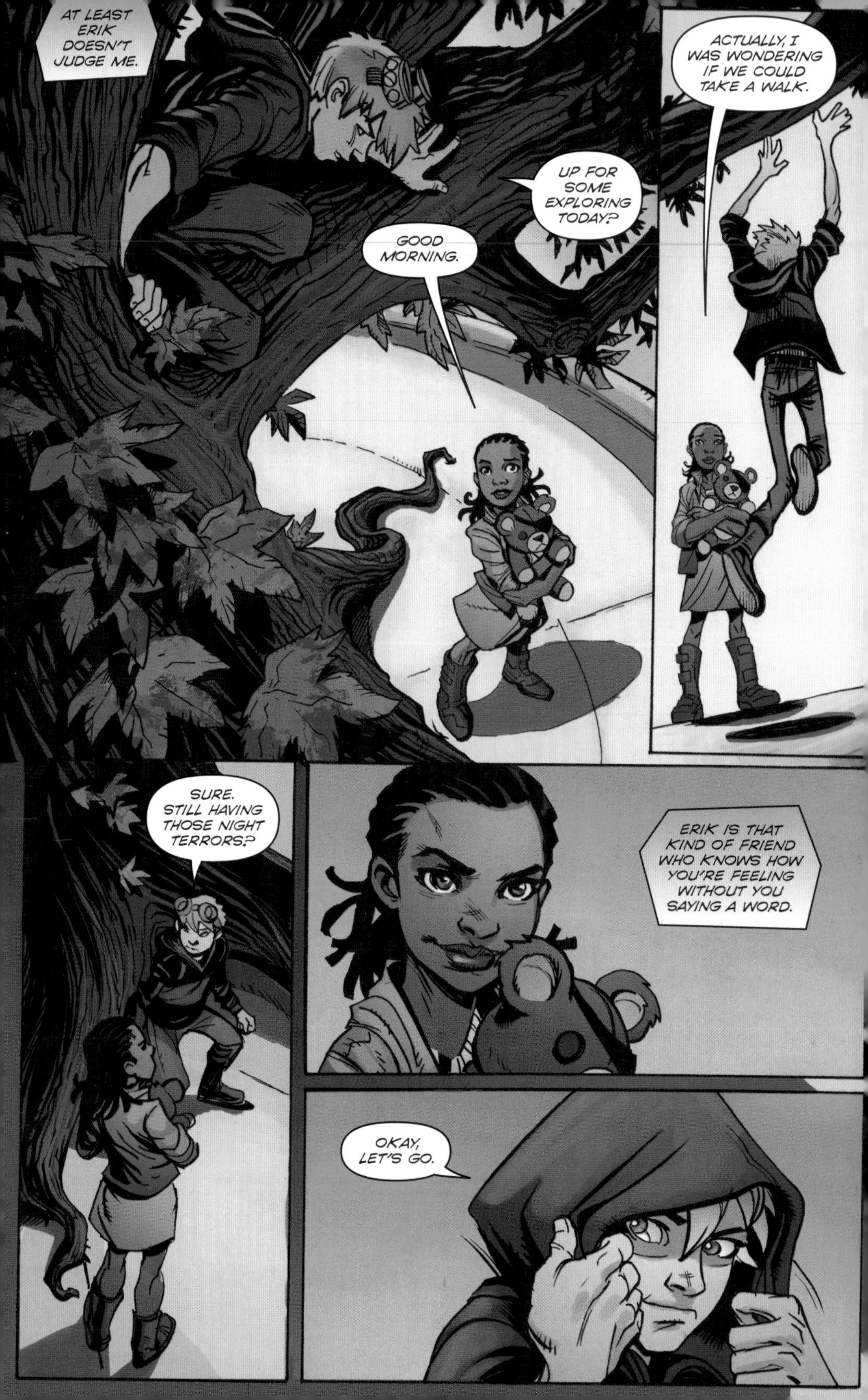
AT LEAST ERIK DOESN'T JUDGE ME.
UP FOR SOME EXPLORING TODAY?
GOOD MORNING.
ACTUALLY, I WAS WONDERING IF WE COULD TAKE A WALK.
SURE. STILL HAVING THOSE NIGHT TERRORS?
ERIK IS THAT KIND OF FRIEND WHO KNOWS HOW YOU'RE FEELING WITHOUT YOU SAYING A WORD.
OKAY, LET'S GO.

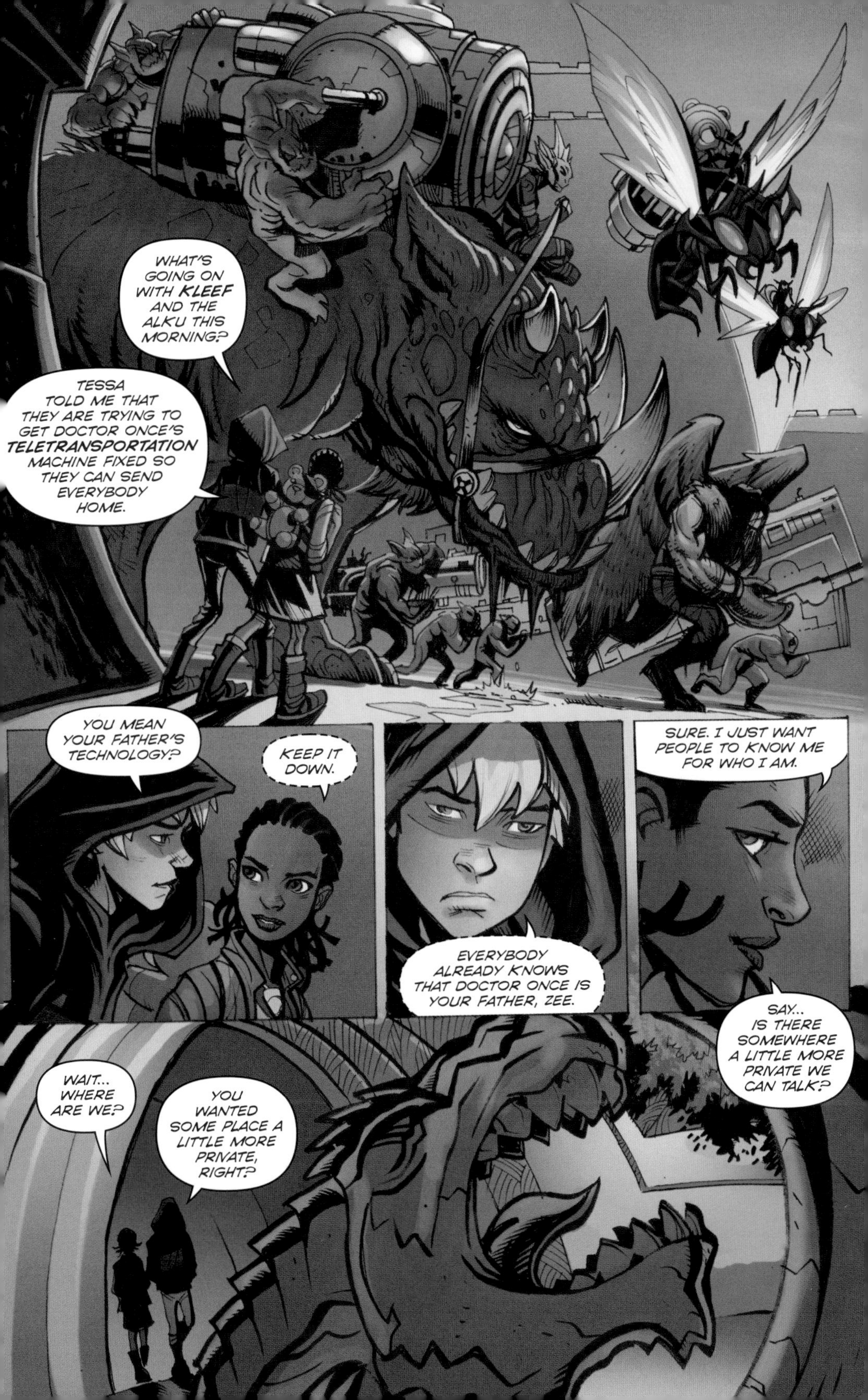
WHAT'S GOING ON WITH KLEEF AND THE ALKU THIS MORNING?
TESSA TOLD ME THAT THEY ARE TRYING TO GET DOCTOR ONCE'S TELETRANSPORTATION MACHINE FIXED SO THEY CAN SEND EVERYBODY HOME.
YOU MEAN YOUR FATHER'S TECHNOLOGY?
KEEP IT DOWN.
EVERYBODY ALREADY KNOWS THAT DOCTOR ONCE IS YOUR FATHER, ZEE.
SURE. I JUST WANT PEOPLE TO KNOW ME FOR WHO I AM.
SAY... IS THERE SOMEWHERE A LITTLE MORE PRIVATE WE CAN TALK?
WAIT... WHERE ARE WE?
YOU WANTED SOME PLACE A LITTLE MORE PRIVATE, RIGHT?

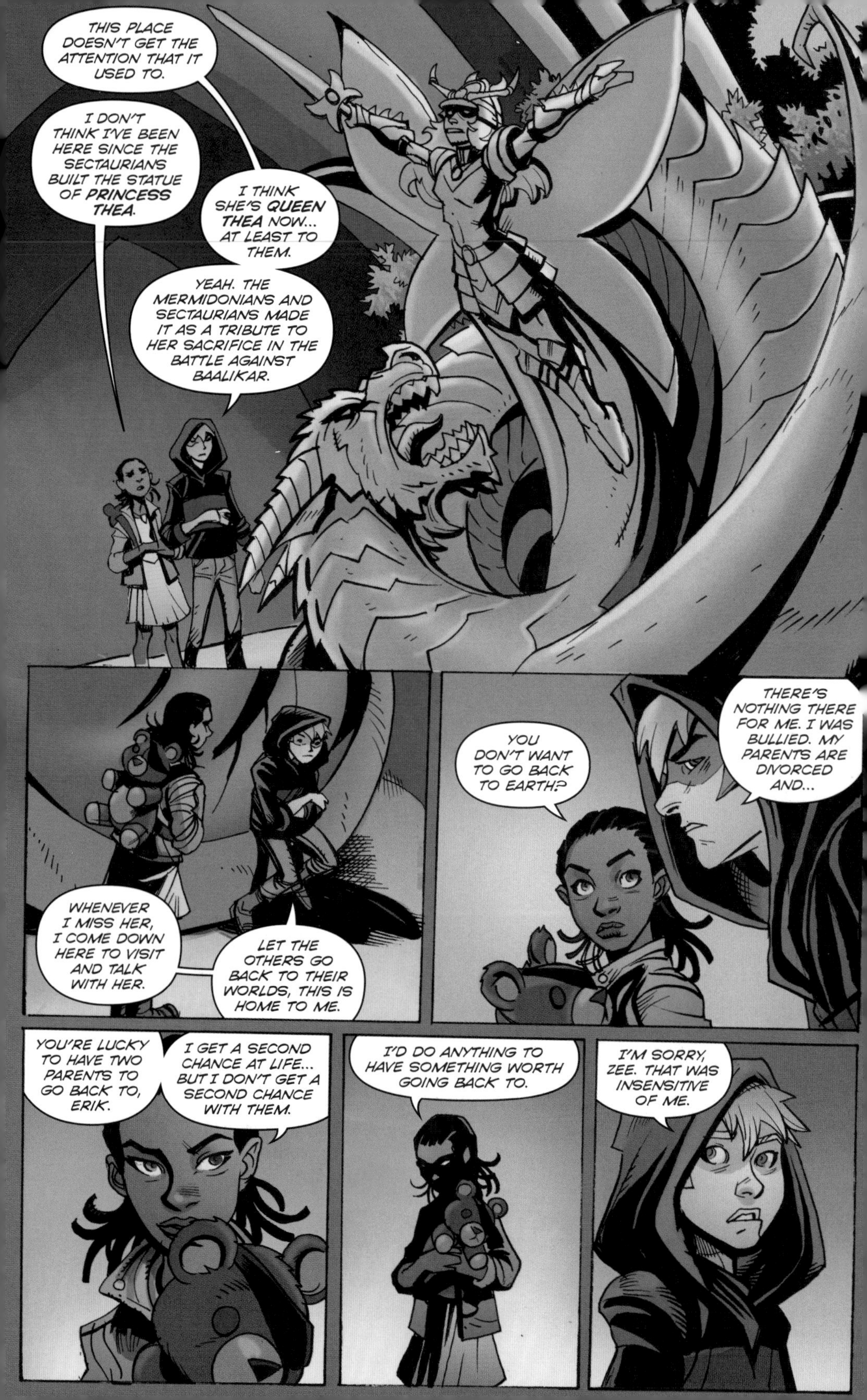
THIS PLACE DOESN'T GET THE ATTENTION THAT IT USED TO.
I DON'T THINK I'VE BEEN HERE SINCE THE SECTAURIANS BUILT THE STATUE OF PRINCESS THEA.
I THINK SHE'S QUEEN THEA NOW... AT LEAST TO THEM.
YEAH. THE MERMIDONIANS AND SECTAURIANS MADE IT AS A TRIBUTE TO HER SACRIFICE IN THE BATTLE AGAINST BAALIKAR.
WHENEVER I MISS HER, I COME DOWN HERE TO VISIT AND TALK WITH HER.
LET THE OTHERS GO BACK TO THEIR WORLDS, THIS IS HOME TO ME.
YOU DON'T WANT TO GO BACK TO EARTH?
THERE'S NOTHING THERE FOR ME. I WAS BULLIED. MY PARENTS ARE DIVORCED AND...
YOU'RE LUCKY TO HAVE TWO PARENTS TO GO BACK TO, ERIK.
I GET A SECOND CHANCE AT LIFE... BUT I DON'T GET A SECOND CHANCE WITH THEM.
I'D DO ANYTHING TO HAVE SOMETHING WORTH GOING BACK TO.
I'M SORRY, ZEE. THAT WAS INSENSITIVE OF ME.

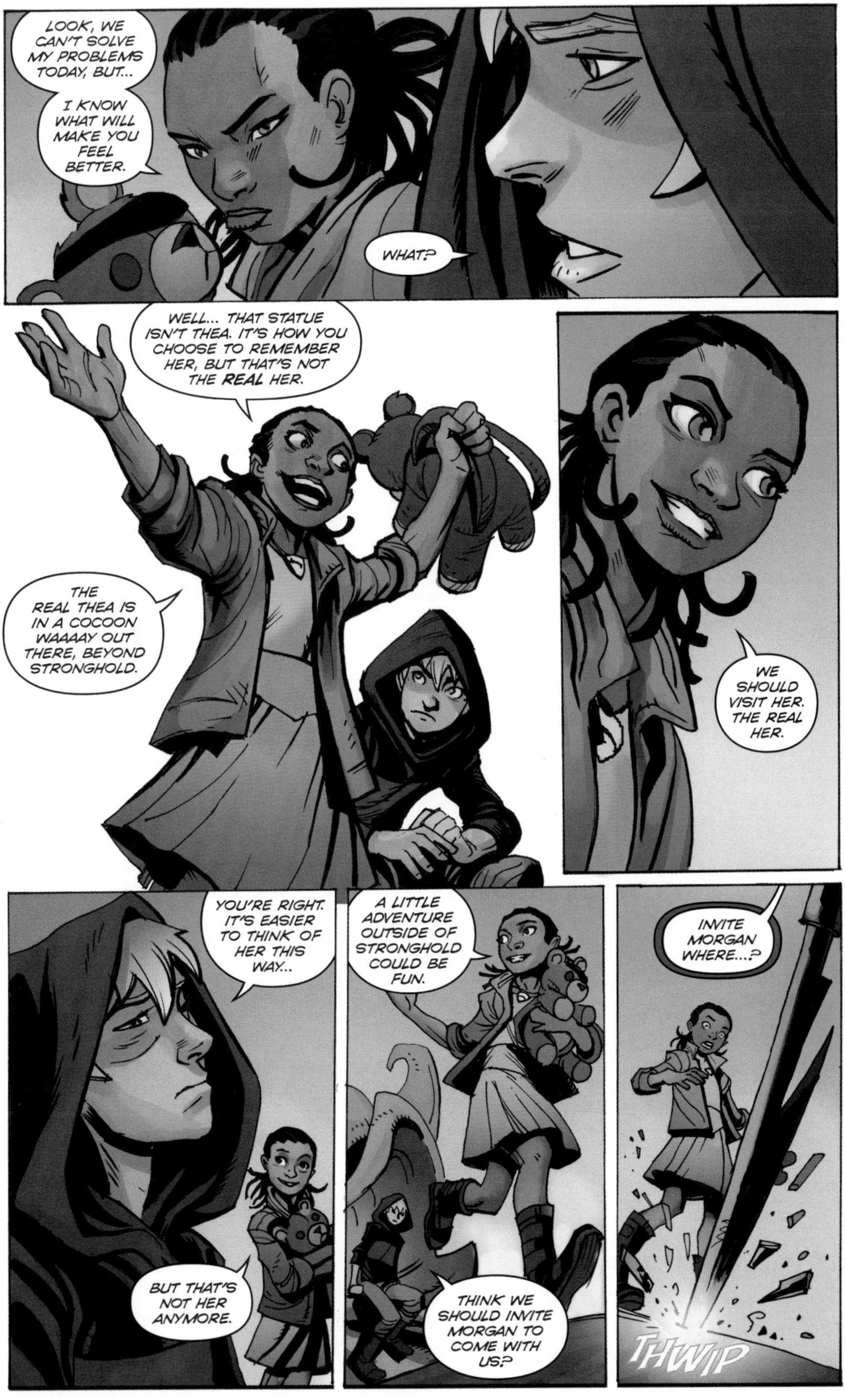
LOOK, WE CAN'T SOLVE MY PROBLEMS TODAY, BUT...
I KNOW WHAT WILL MAKE YOU FEEL BETTER.
WHAT?
WELL... THAT STATUE ISN'T THEA. IT'S HOW YOU CHOOSE TO REMEMBER HER, BUT THAT'S NOT THE REAL HER.
THE REAL THEA IS IN A COCOON WAAAAY OUT THERE, BEYOND STRONGHOLD.
WE SHOULD VISIT HER. THE REAL HER.
YOU'RE RIGHT. IT'S EASIER TO THINK OF HER THIS WAY...
BUT THAT'S NOT HER ANYMORE.
A LITTLE ADVENTURE OUTSIDE OF STRONGHOLD COULD BE FUN.
THINK WE SHOULD INVITE MORGAN TO COME WITH US?
INVITE MORGAN WHERE...?
THWIP

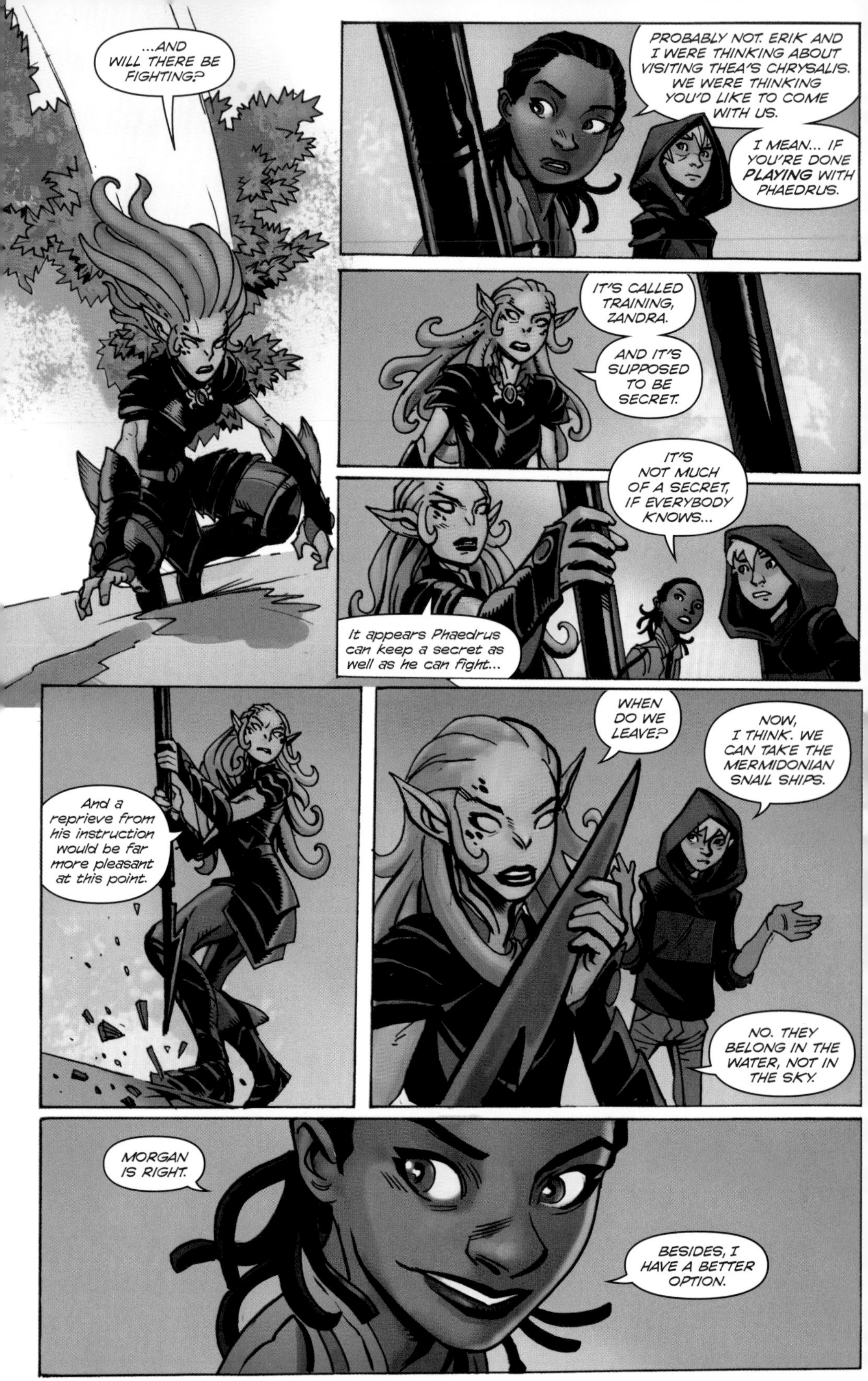
...AND WILL THERE BE FIGHTING?
PROBABLY NOT. ERIK AND I WERE THINKING ABOUT VISITING THEA'S CHRYSALIS. WE WERE THINKING YOU'D LIKE TO COME WITH US.
I MEAN... IF YOU'RE DONE PLAYING WITH PHAEDRUS.
IT'S CALLED TRAINING, ZANDRA.
AND IT'S SUPPOSED TO BE SECRET.
IT'S NOT MUCH OF A SECRET, IF EVERYBODY KNOWS...
It appears Phaedrus can keep a secret as well as he can fight...
And a reprieve from his instruction would be far more pleasant at this point.
WHEN DO WE LEAVE?
NOW, I THINK. WE CAN TAKE THE MERMIDONIAN SNAIL SHIPS.
NO. THEY BELONG IN THE WATER, NOT IN THE SKY.
MORGAN IS RIGHT.
BESIDES, I HAVE A BETTER OPTION.

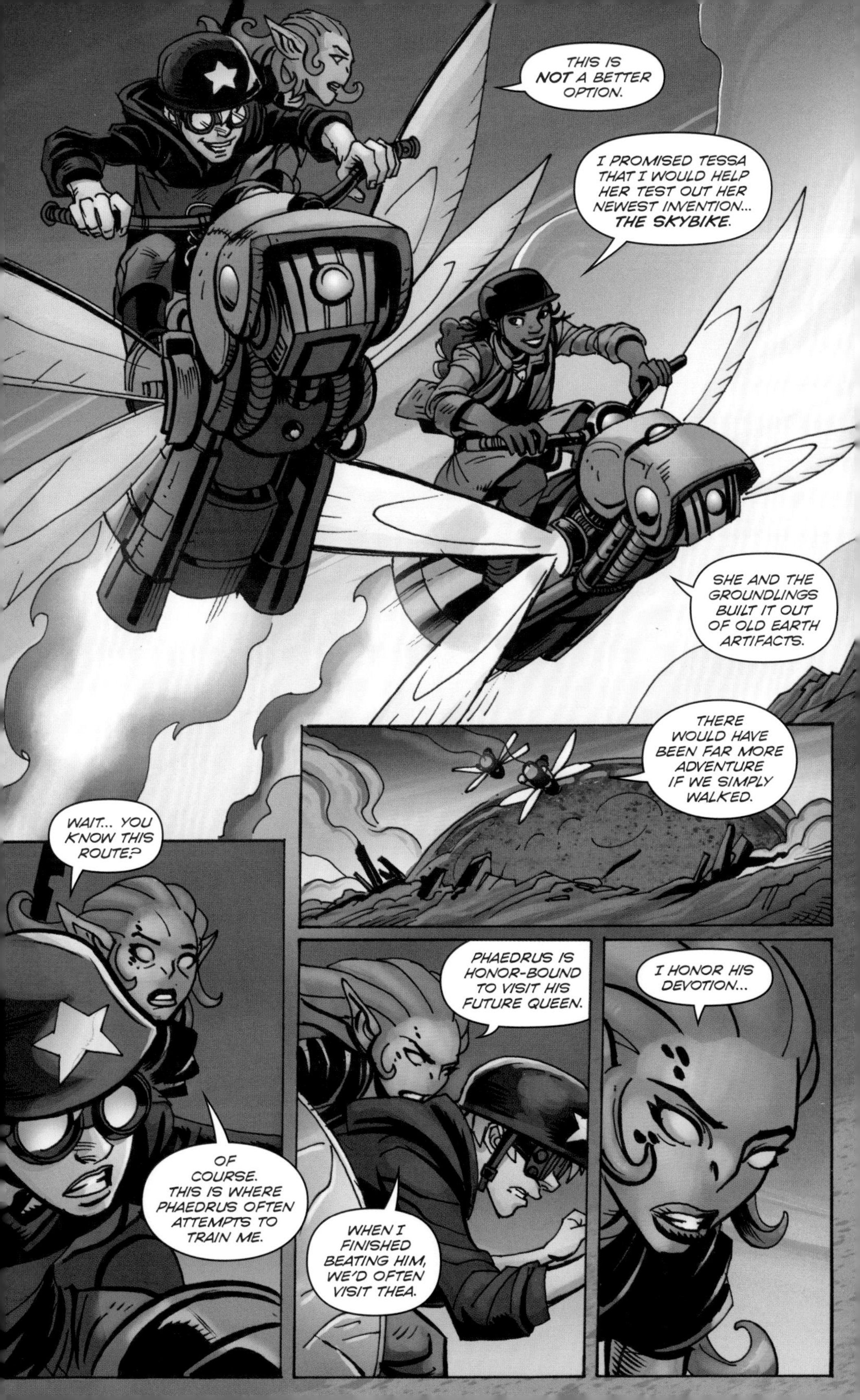
THIS IS NOT A BETTER OPTION.
I PROMISED TESSA THAT I WOULD HELP HER TEST OUT HER NEWEST INVENTION... THE SKYBIKE.
SHE AND THE GROUNDLINGS BUILT IT OUT OF OLD EARTH ARTIFACTS.
THERE WOULD HAVE BEEN FAR MORE ADVENTURE IF WE SIMPLY WALKED.
WAIT... YOU KNOW THIS ROUTE?
OF COURSE. THIS IS WHERE PHAEDRUS OFTEN ATTEMPTS TO TRAIN ME.
PHAEDRUS IS HONOR-BOUND TO VISIT HIS FUTURE QUEEN.
WHEN I FINISHED BEATING HIM, WE'D OFTEN VISIT THEA.
I HONOR HIS DEVOTION...

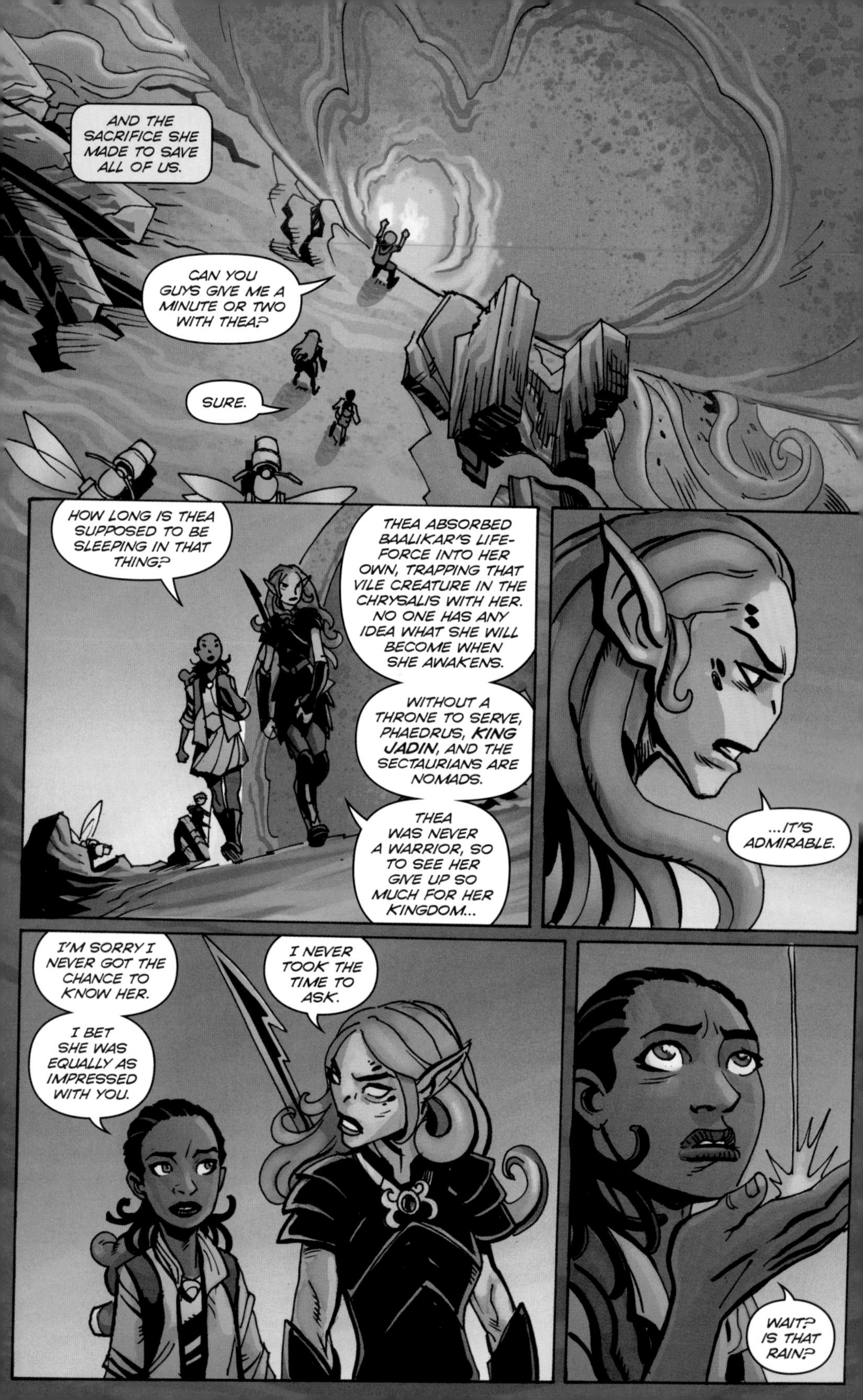
AND THE SACRIFICE SHE MADE TO SAVE ALL OF US.
CAN YOU GUYS GIVE ME A MINUTE OR TWO WITH THEA?
SURE.
HOW LONG IS THEA SUPPOSED TO BE SLEEPING IN THAT THING?
THEA ABSORBED BAALIKAR'S LIFE-FORCE INTO HER OWN, TRAPPING THAT VILE CREATURE IN THE CHRYSALIS WITH HER. NO ONE HAS ANY IDEA WHAT SHE WILL BECOME WHEN SHE AWAKENS.
WITHOUT A THRONE TO SERVE, PHAEDRUS, KING JADIN, AND THE SECTAURIANS ARE NOMADS.
THEA WAS NEVER A WARRIOR, SO TO SEE HER GIVE UP SO MUCH FOR HER KINGDOM...
...IT'S ADMIRABLE.
I'M SORRY I NEVER GOT THE CHANCE TO KNOW HER.
I BET SHE WAS EQUALLY AS IMPRESSED WITH YOU.
I NEVER TOOK THE TIME TO ASK.
WAIT? IS THAT RAIN?

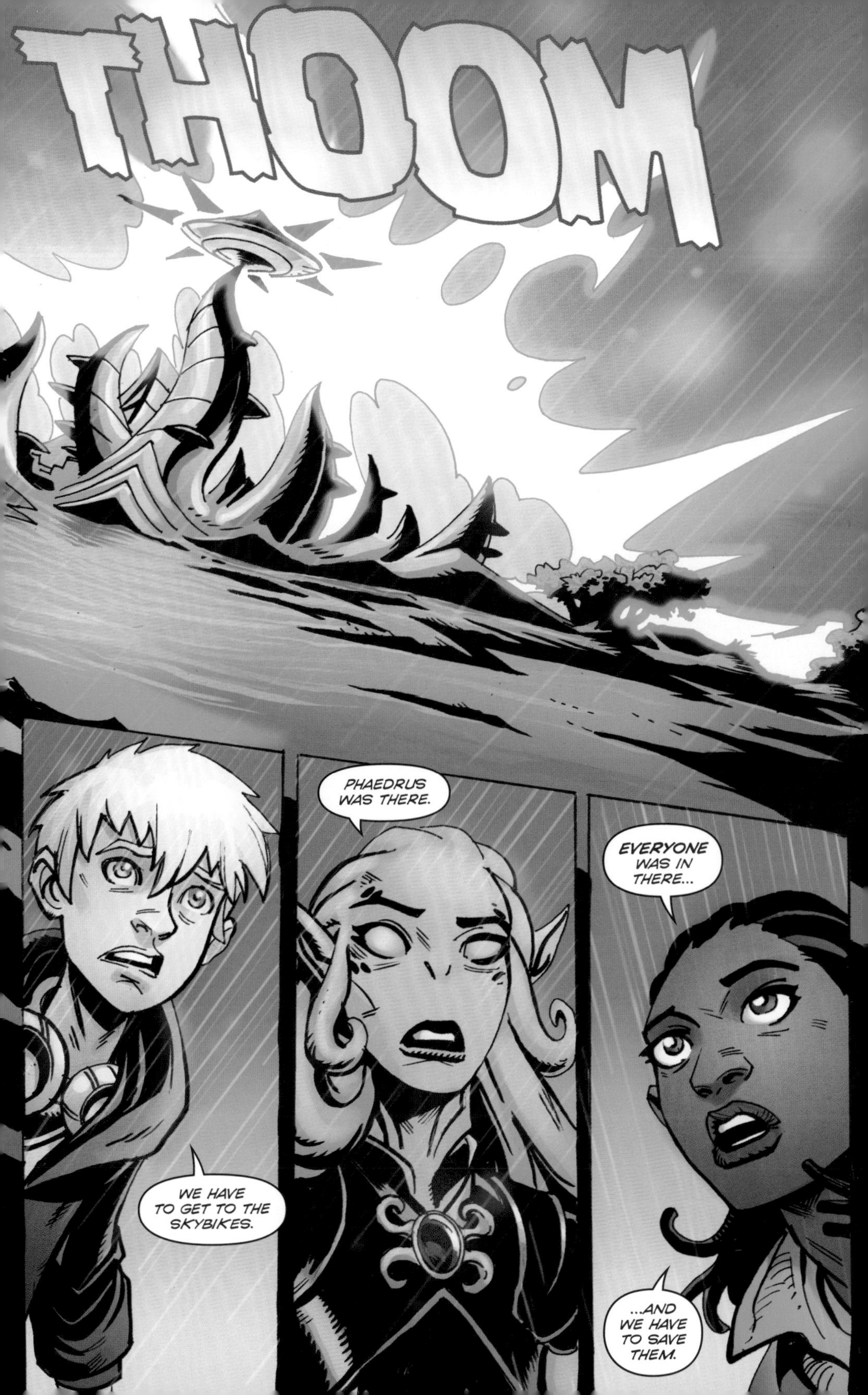
THOOM
PHAEDRUS WAS THERE.
EVERYONE WAS IN THERE...
WE HAVE TO GET TO THE SKYBIKES.
...AND WE HAVE TO SAVE THEM.

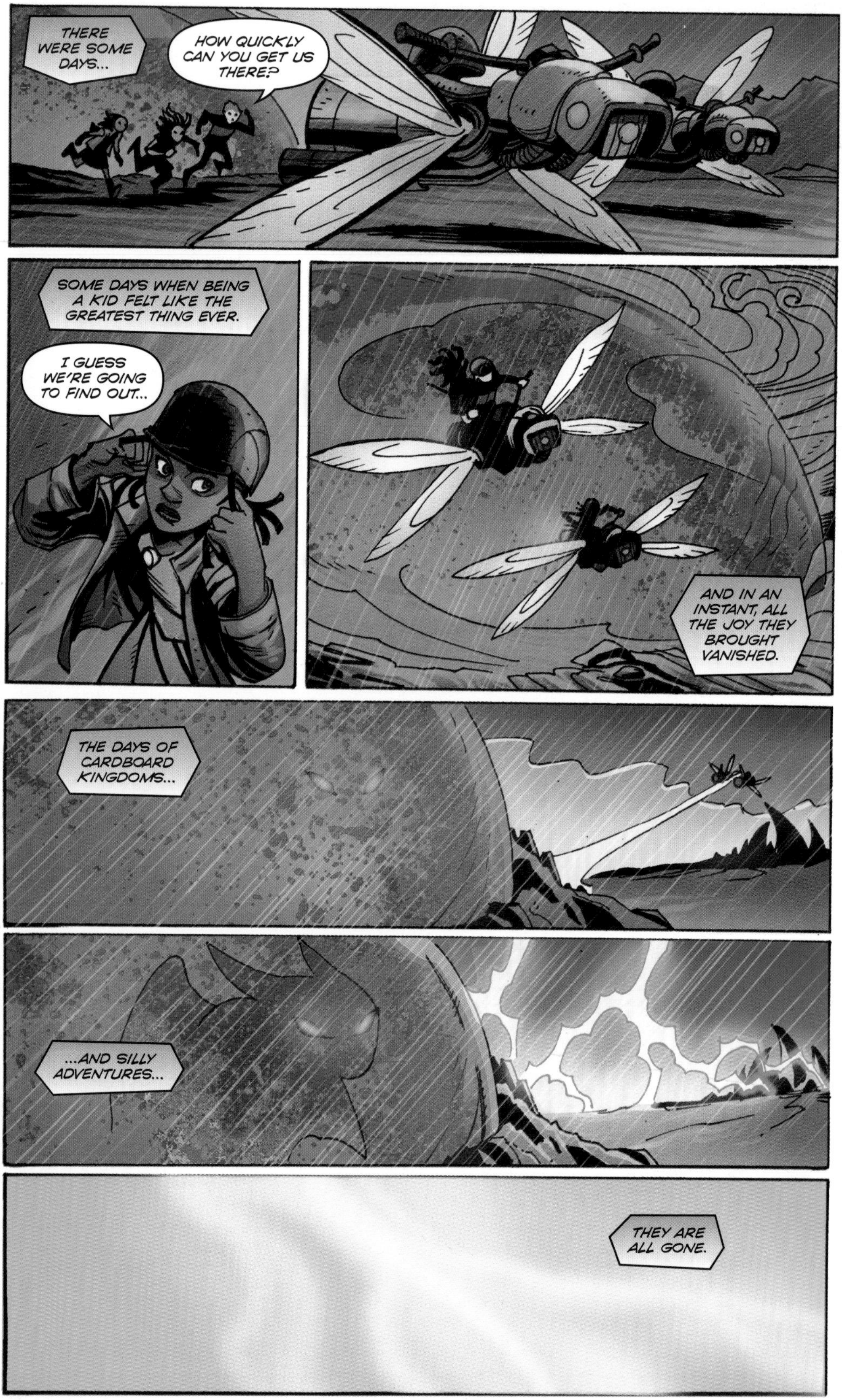
THERE WERE SOME DAYS...
HOW QUICKLY CAN YOU GET US THERE?
SOME DAYS WHEN BEING A KID FELT LIKE THE GREATEST THING EVER.
I GUESS WE'RE GOING TO FIND OUT...
AND IN AN INSTANT, ALL THE JOY THEY BROUGHT VANISHED.
THE DAYS OF CARDBOARD KINGDOMS...
...AND SILLY ADVENTURES...
THEY ARE ALL GONE.

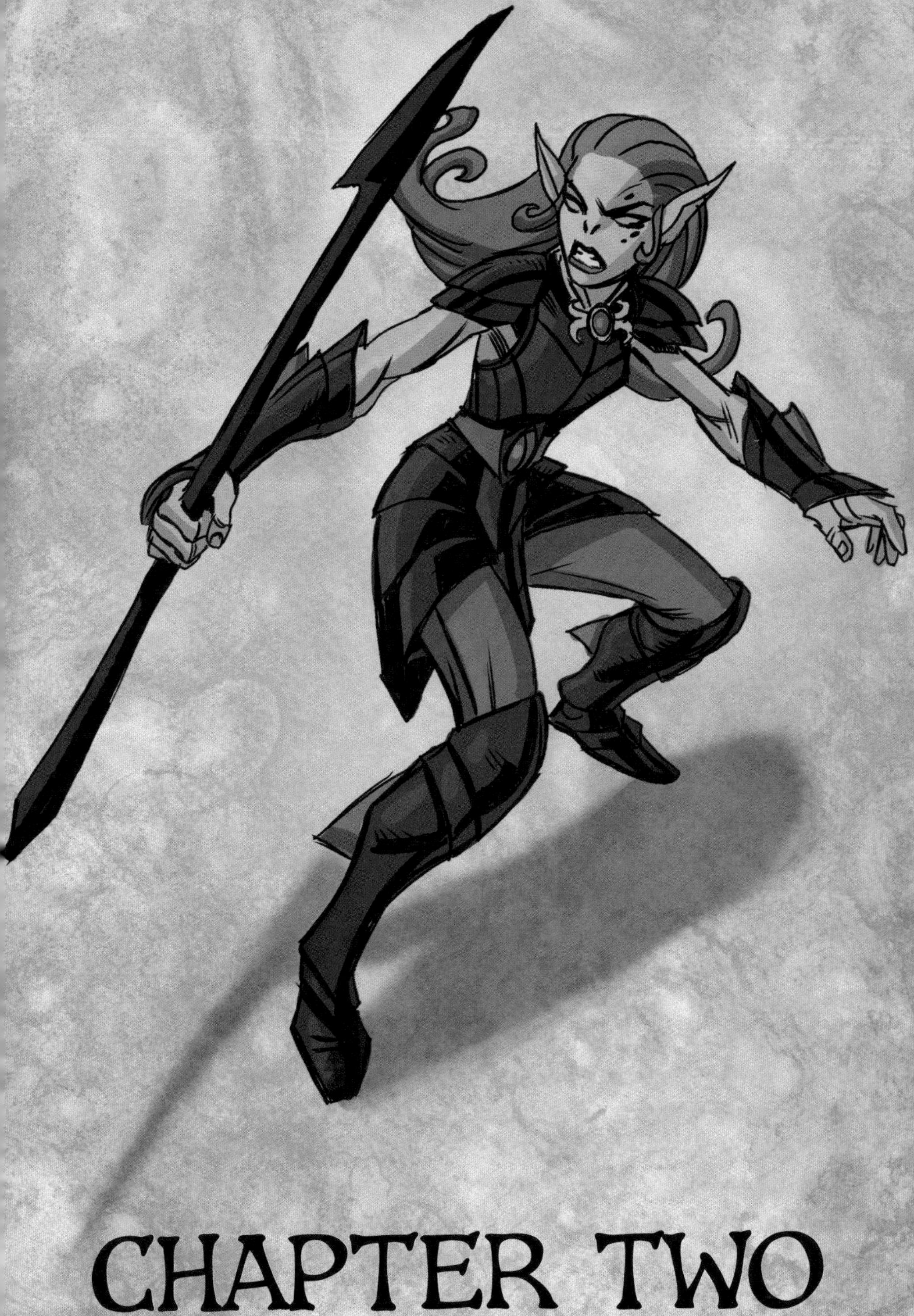

CHAPTER TWO

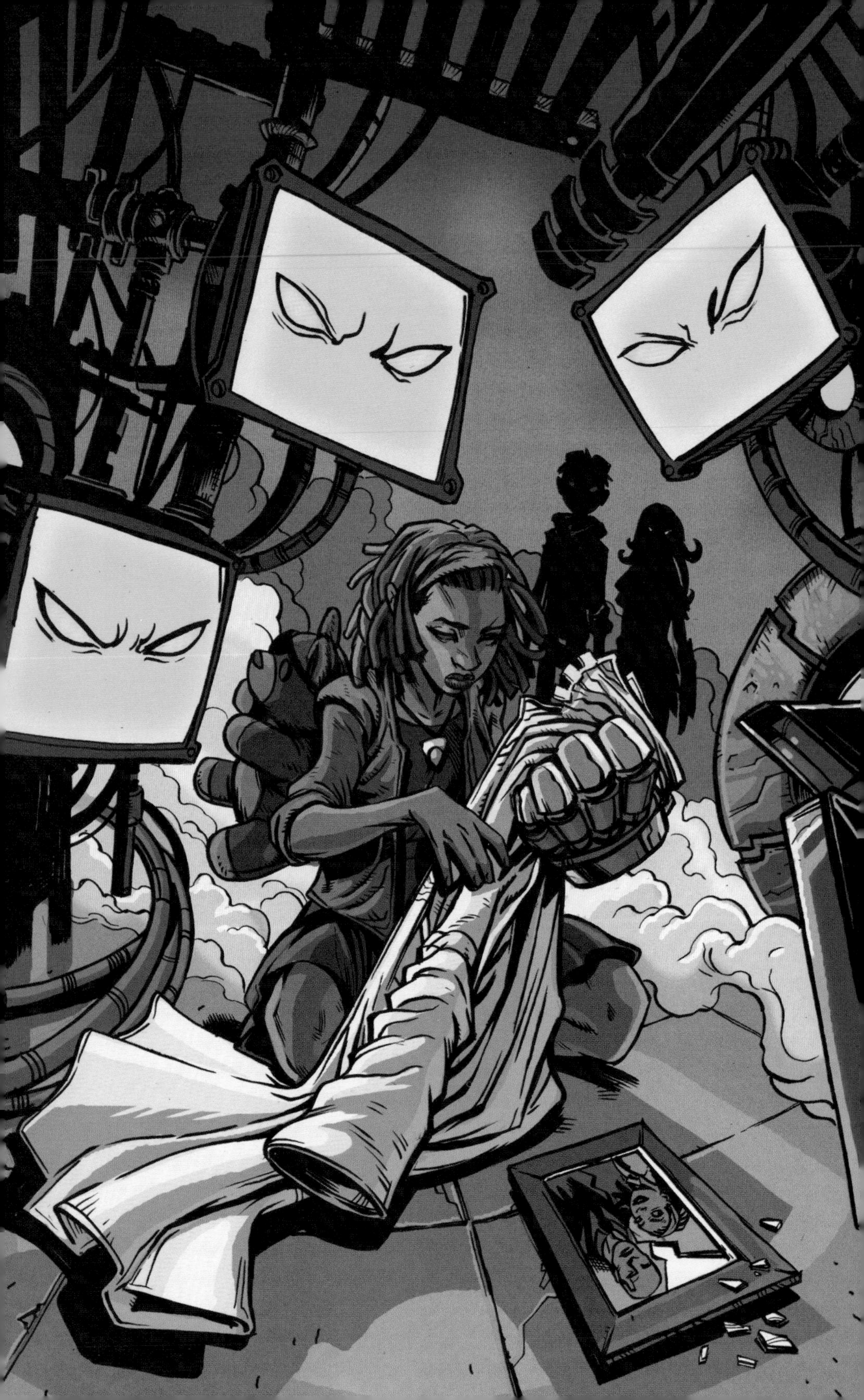

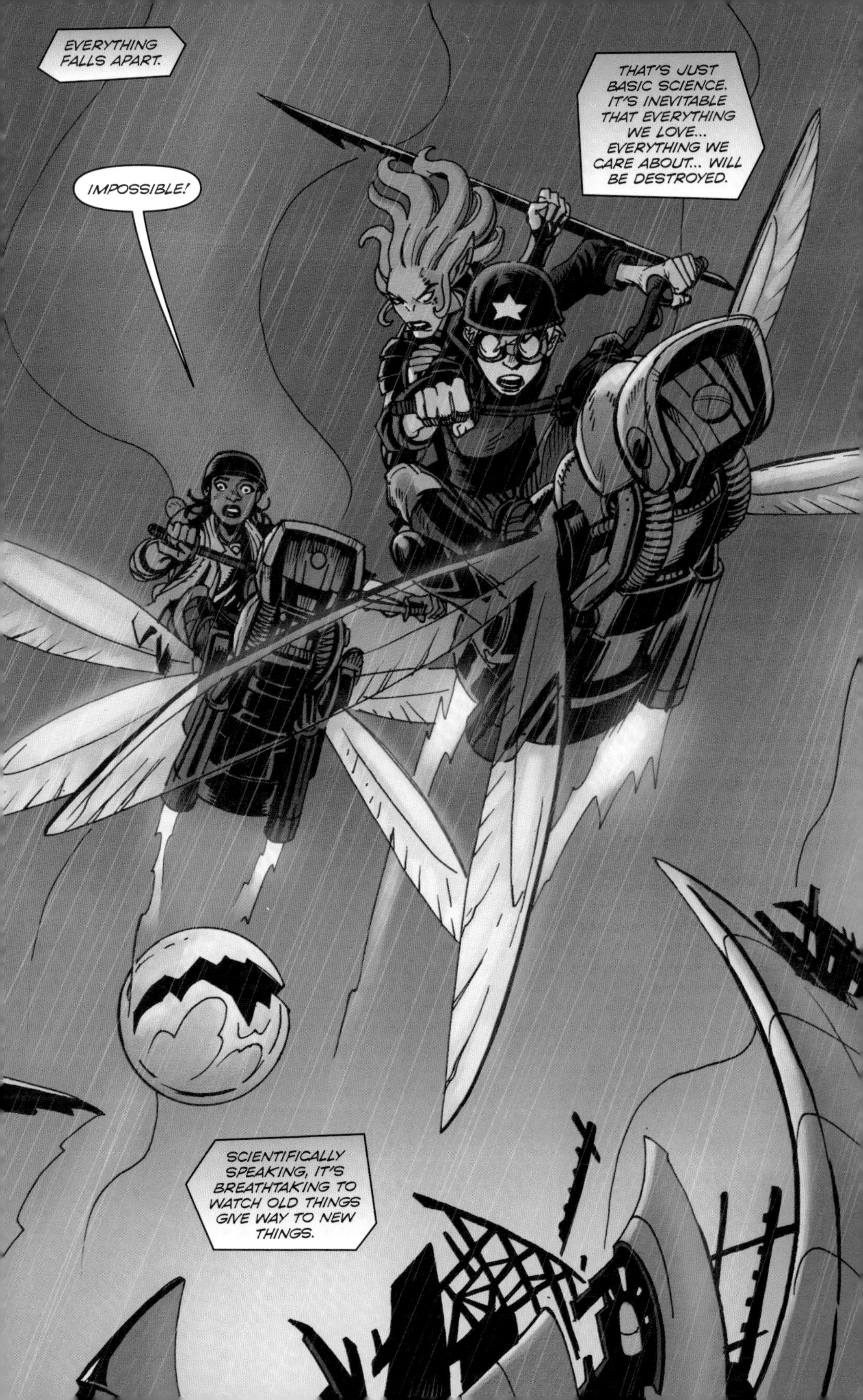
EVERYTHING FALLS APART.
THAT'S JUST BASIC SCIENCE. IT'S INEVITABLE THAT EVERYTHING WE LOVE... EVERYTHING WE CARE ABOUT... WILL BE DESTROYED.
IMPOSSIBLE!
SCIENTIFICALLY SPEAKING, IT'S BREATHTAKING TO WATCH OLD THINGS GIVE WAY TO NEW THINGS.

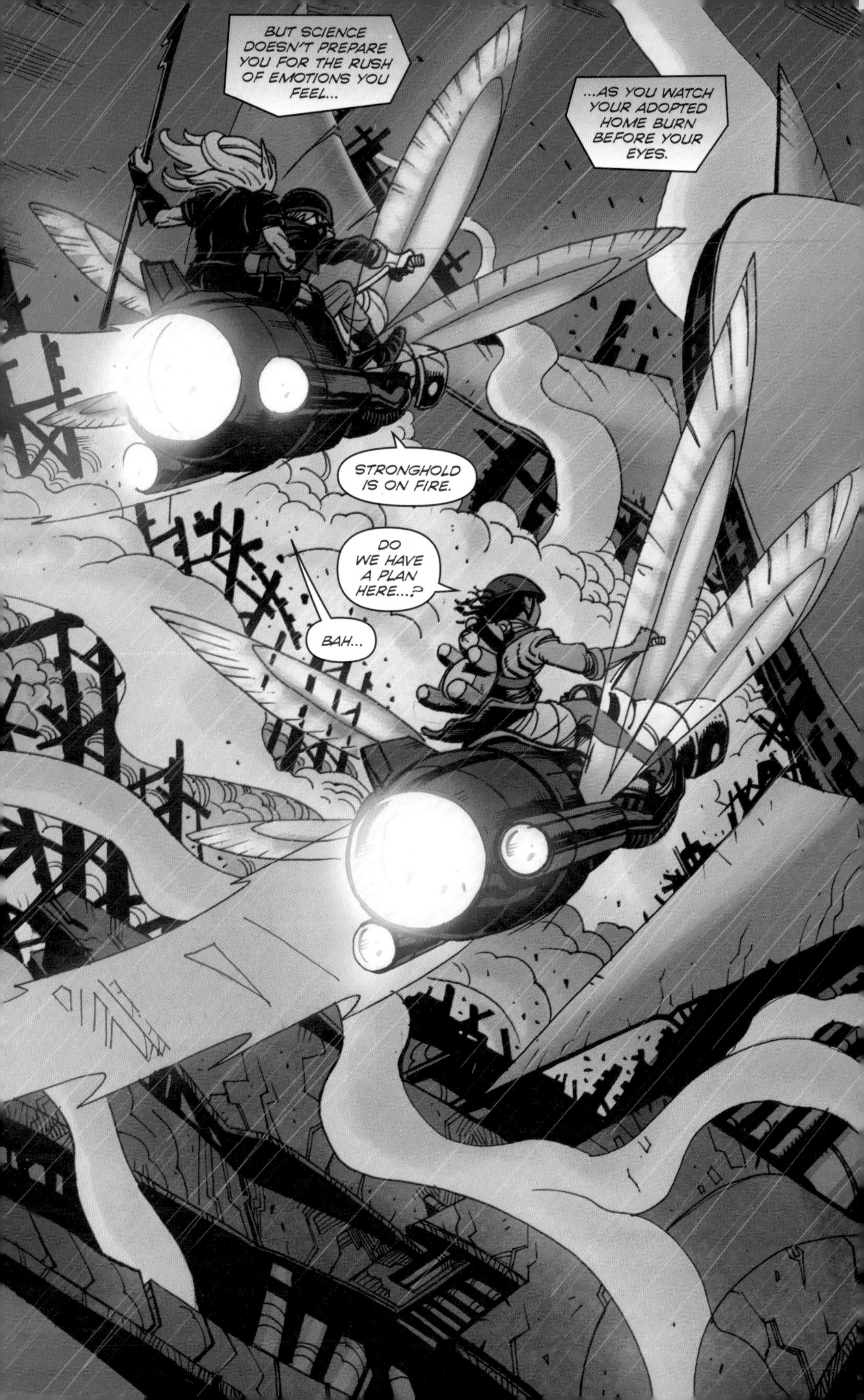
BUT SCIENCE DOESN'T PREPARE YOU FOR THE RUSH OF EMOTIONS YOU FEEL...
...AS YOU WATCH YOUR ADOPTED HOME BURN BEFORE YOUR EYES.
STRONGHOLD IS ON FIRE.
DO WE HAVE A PLAN HERE...?
BAH...

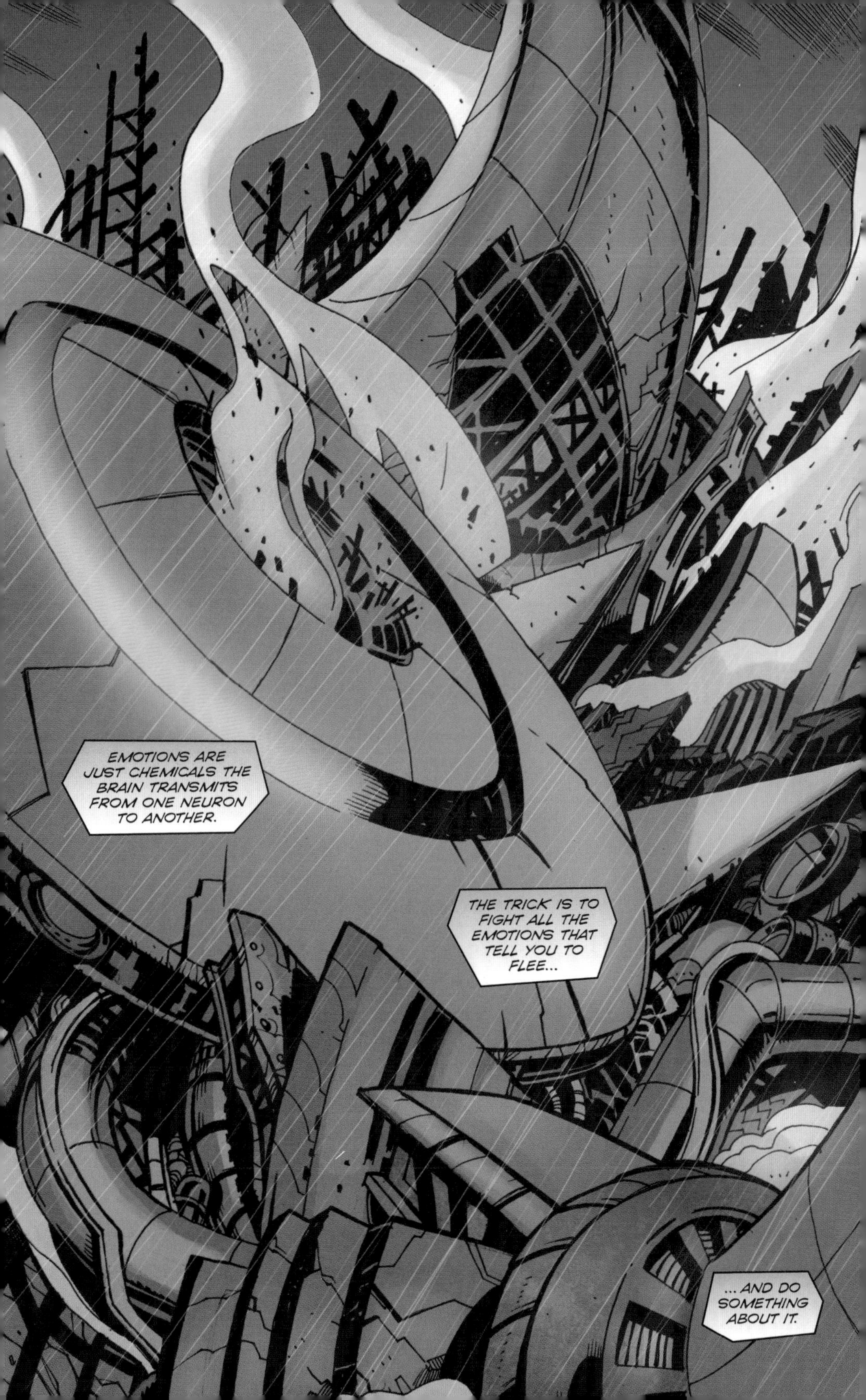
EMOTIONS ARE JUST CHEMICALS THE BRAIN TRANSMITS FROM ONE NEURON TO ANOTHER.
THE TRICK IS TO FIGHT ALL THE EMOTIONS THAT TELL YOU TO FLEE...
...AND DO SOMETHING ABOUT IT.

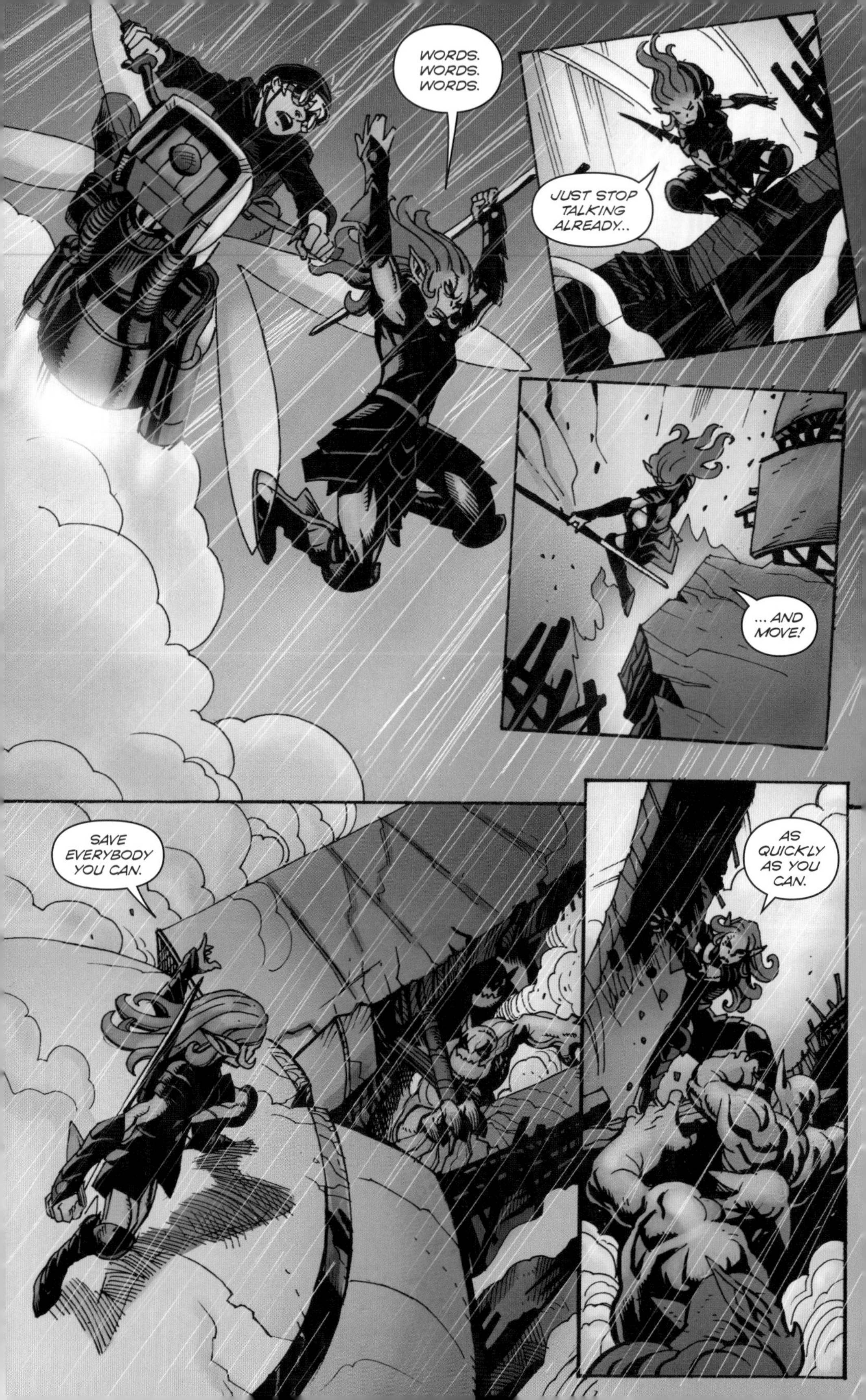
WORDS.
WORDS.
WORDS.
JUST STOP TALKING ALREADY...
...AND MOVE!
SAVE EVERYBODY YOU CAN.
AS QUICKLY AS YOU CAN.

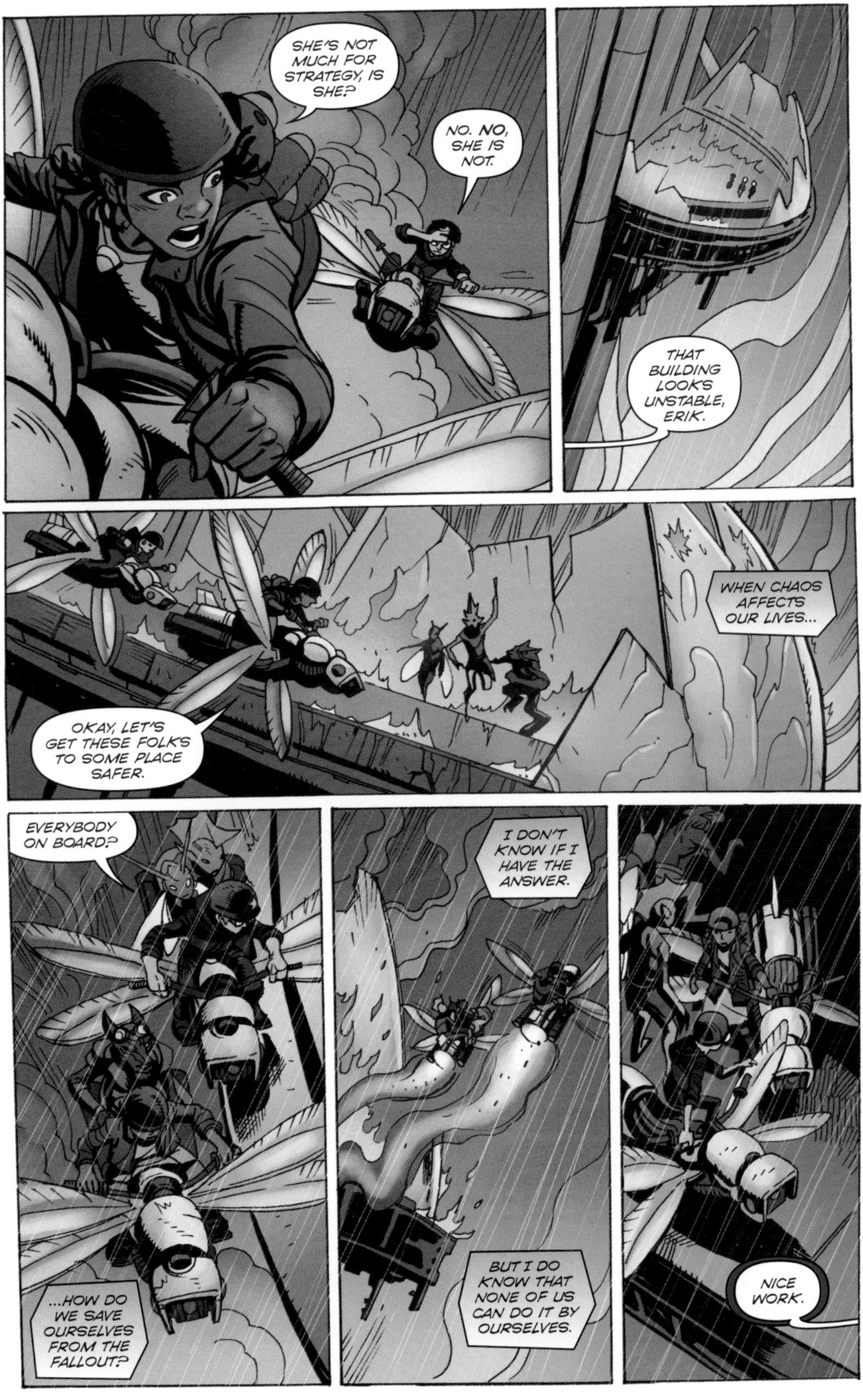
SHE'S NOT MUCH FOR STRATEGY, IS SHE?
NO. NO, SHE IS NOT.
THAT BUILDING LOOKS UNSTABLE, ERIK.
WHEN CHAOS AFFECTS OUR LIVES...
OKAY, LET'S GET THESE FOLKS TO SOME PLACE SAFER.
EVERYBODY ON BOARD?
...HOW DO WE SAVE OURSELVES FROM THE FALLOUT?
I DON'T KNOW IF I HAVE THE ANSWER.
BUT I DO KNOW THAT NONE OF US CAN DO IT BY OURSELVES.
NICE WORK.

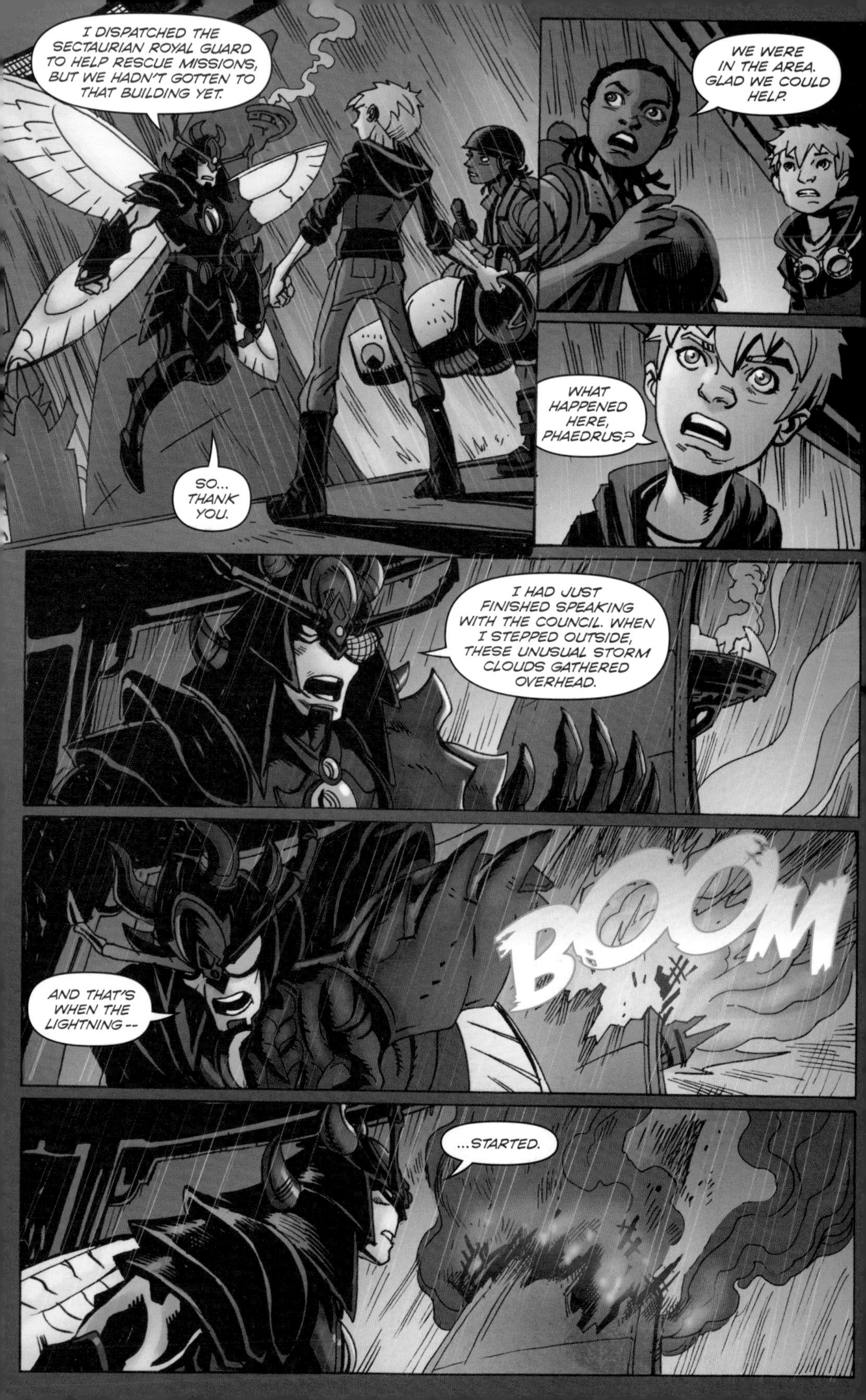
I DISPATCHED THE SECTAURIAN ROYAL GUARD TO HELP RESCUE MISSIONS, BUT WE HADN'T GOTTEN TO THAT BUILDING YET.
SO... THANK YOU.
WE WERE IN THE AREA. GLAD WE COULD HELP.
WHAT HAPPENED HERE, PHAEDRUS?
I HAD JUST FINISHED SPEAKING WITH THE COUNCIL. WHEN I STEPPED OUTSIDE, THESE UNUSUAL STORM CLOUDS GATHERED OVERHEAD.
AND THAT'S WHEN THE LIGHTNING --
BOOM
...STARTED.

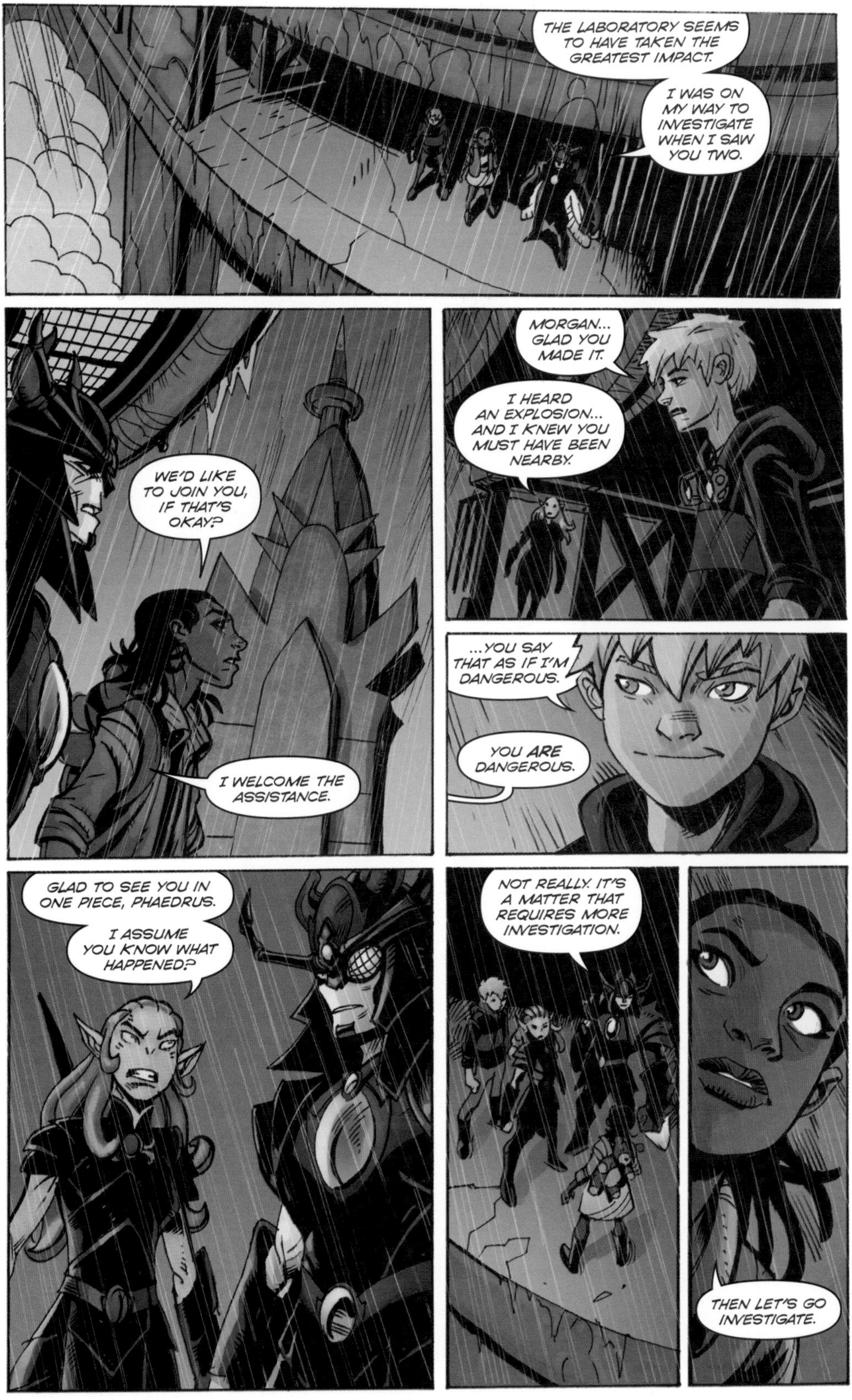
THE LABORATORY SEEMS TO HAVE TAKEN THE GREATEST IMPACT.
I WAS ON MY WAY TO INVESTIGATE WHEN I SAW YOU TWO.
WE'D LIKE TO JOIN YOU, IF THAT'S OKAY?
I WELCOME THE ASSISTANCE.
MORGAN... GLAD YOU MADE IT.
I HEARD AN EXPLOSION... AND I KNEW YOU MUST HAVE BEEN NEARBY.
...YOU SAY THAT AS IF I'M DANGEROUS.
YOU ARE DANGEROUS.
GLAD TO SEE YOU IN ONE PIECE, PHAEDRUS.
I ASSUME YOU KNOW WHAT HAPPENED?
NOT REALLY. IT'S A MATTER THAT REQUIRES MORE INVESTIGATION.
THEN LET'S GO INVESTIGATE.

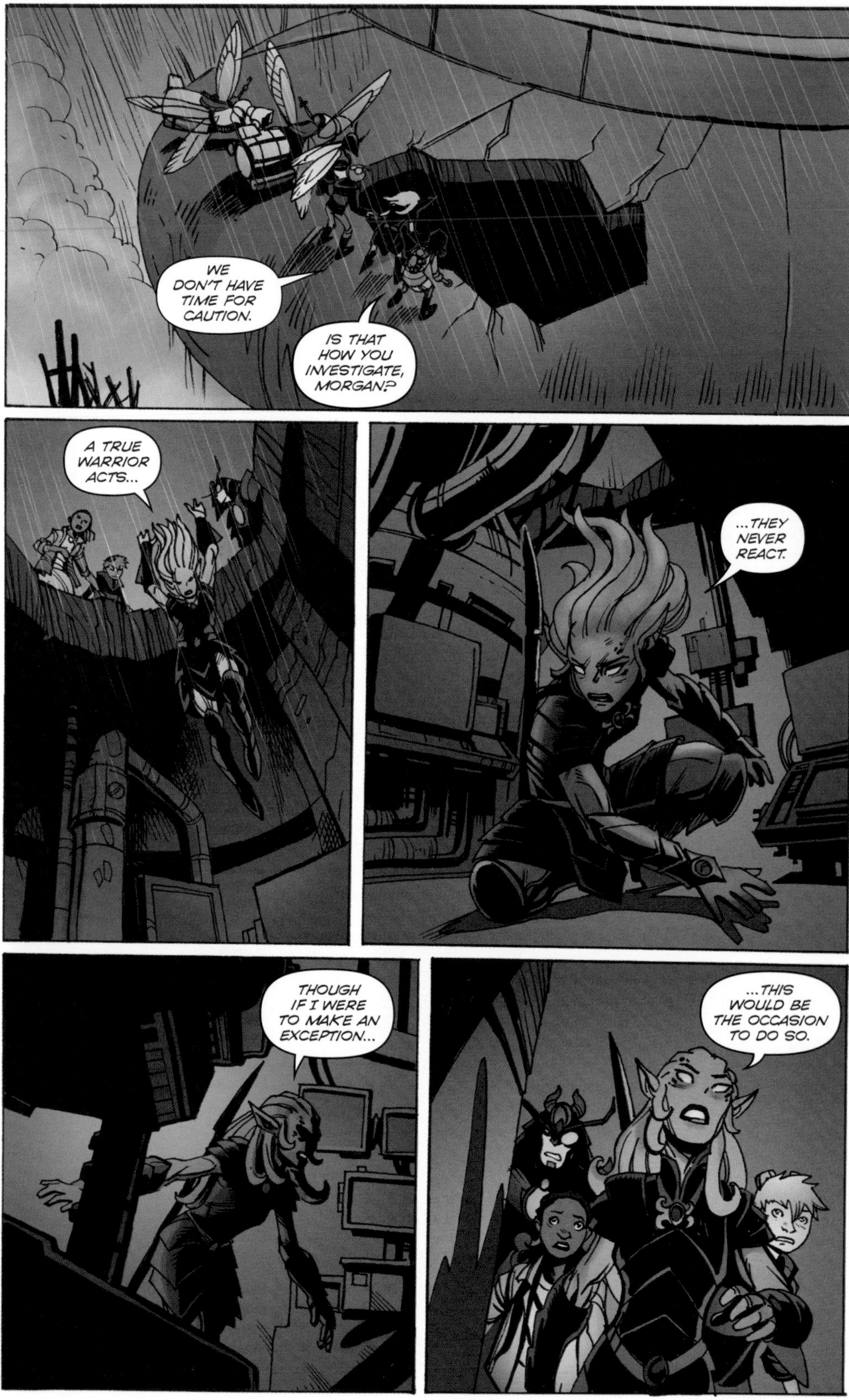
WE DON'T HAVE TIME FOR CAUTION.
IS THAT HOW YOU INVESTIGATE, MORGAN?
A TRUE WARRIOR ACTS...
...THEY NEVER REACT.
THOUGH IF I WERE TO MAKE AN EXCEPTION...
...THIS WOULD BE THE OCCASION TO DO SO.

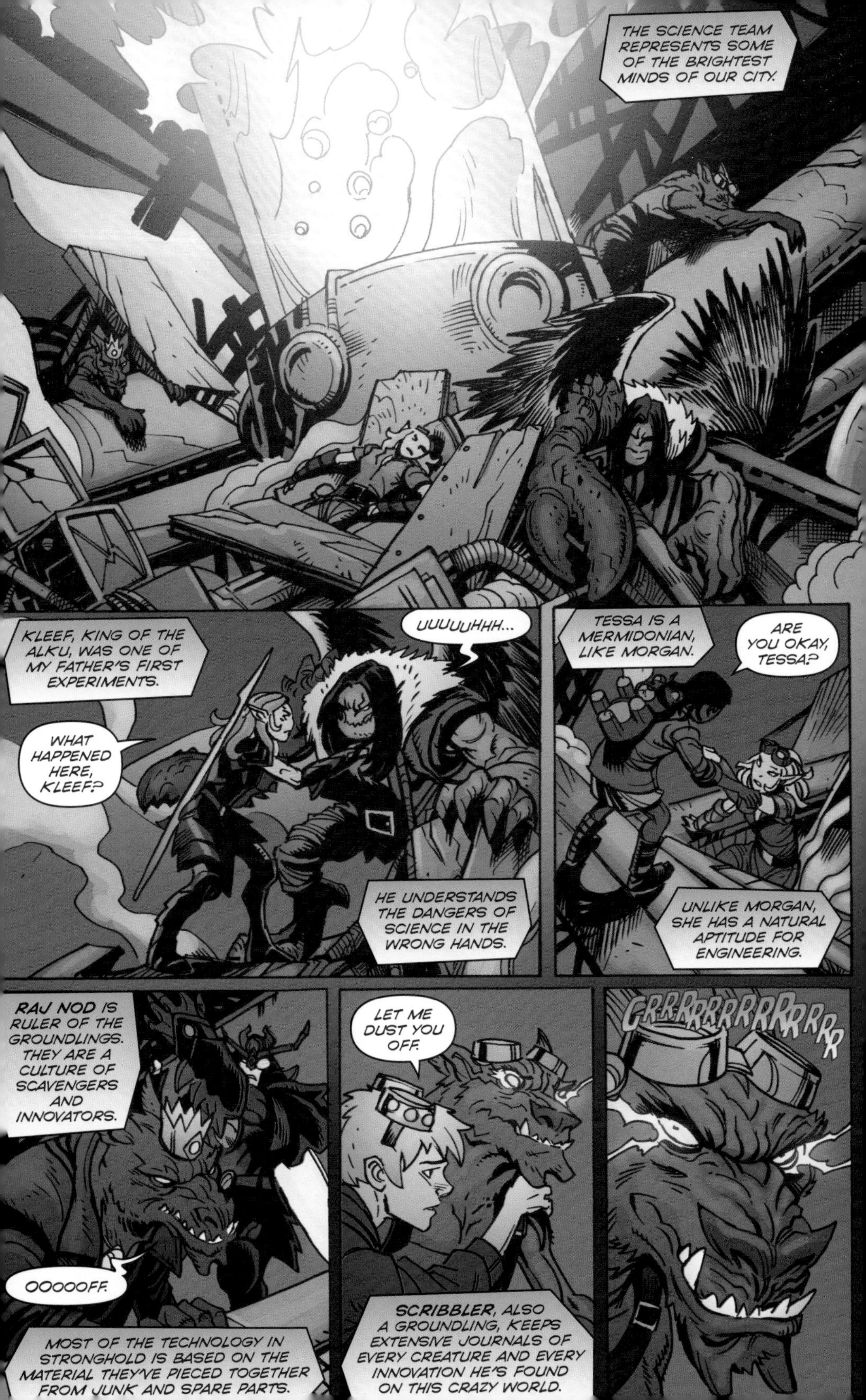
THE SCIENCE TEAM REPRESENTS SOME OF THE BRIGHTEST MINDS OF OUR CITY.
KLEEF, KING OF THE ALKU, WAS ONE OF MY FATHER'S FIRST EXPERIMENTS.
UUUUUHHH...
WHAT HAPPENED HERE, KLEEF?
HE UNDERSTANDS THE DANGERS OF SCIENCE IN THE WRONG HANDS.
TESSA IS A MERMIDONIAN, LIKE MORGAN.
ARE YOU OKAY, TESSA?
UNLIKE MORGAN, SHE HAS A NATURAL APTITUDE FOR ENGINEERING.
RAJ NOD IS RULER OF THE GROUNDLINGS. THEY ARE A CULTURE OF SCAVENGERS AND INNOVATORS.
OOOOOFF.
MOST OF THE TECHNOLOGY IN STRONGHOLD IS BASED ON THE MATERIAL THEY'VE PIECED TOGETHER FROM JUNK AND SPARE PARTS.
LET ME DUST YOU OFF.
SCRIBBLER, ALSO A GROUNDLING, KEEPS EXTENSIVE JOURNALS OF EVERY CREATURE AND EVERY INNOVATION HE'S FOUND ON THIS CRAZY WORLD.
GRRRRRRRRRRRRR

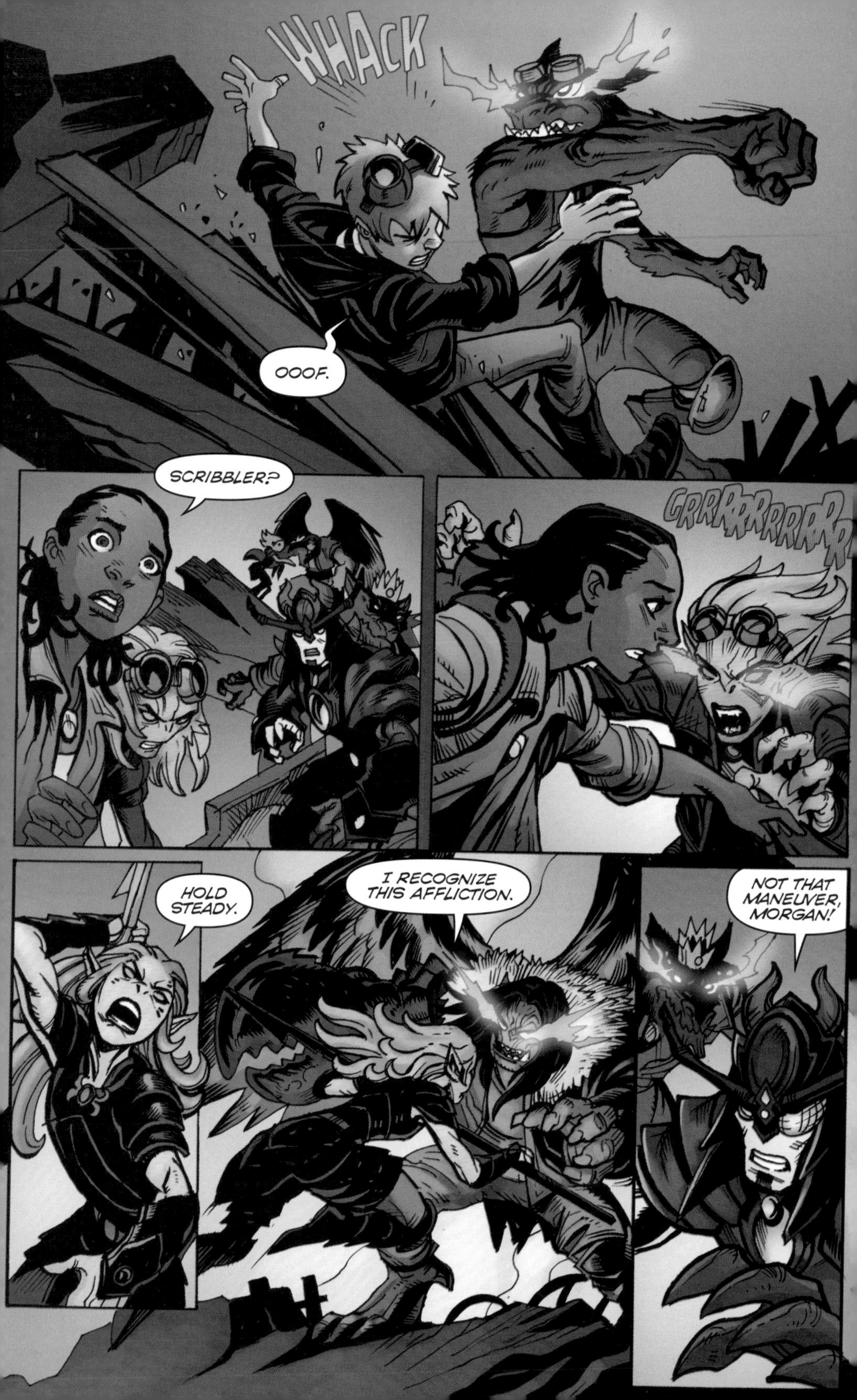
WHACK
OOOF.
SCRIBBLER?
GRRRRRRRRRR
HOLD STEADY.
I RECOGNIZE THIS AFFLICTION.
NOT THAT MANEUVER, MORGAN!

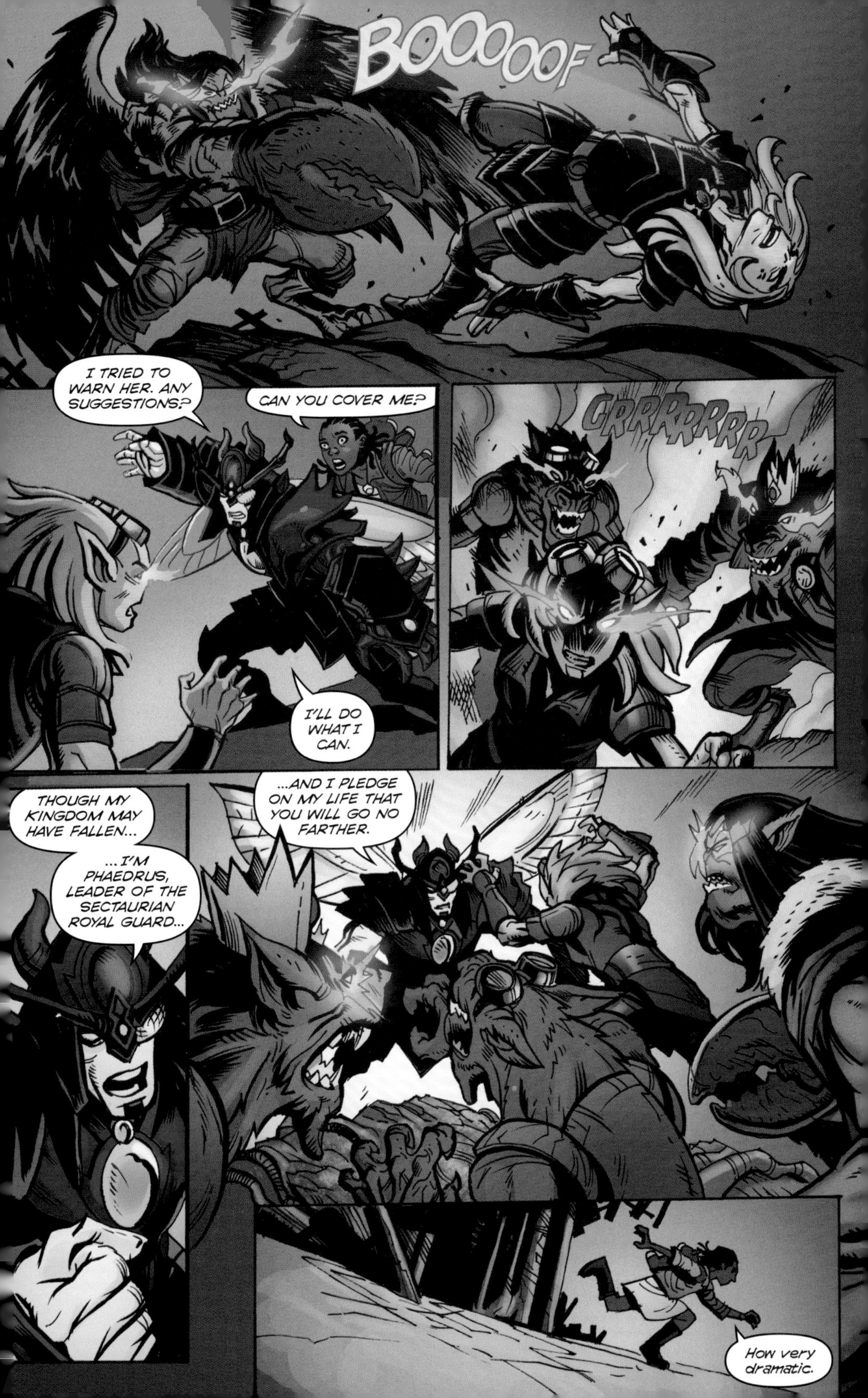
BOOOOOOF
I TRIED TO WARN HER. ANY SUGGESTIONS?
CAN YOU COVER ME?
I'LL DO WHAT I CAN.
GRRRRRRR
THOUGH MY KINGDOM MAY HAVE FALLEN...
...I'M PHAEDRUS, LEADER OF THE SECTAURIAN ROYAL GUARD...
...AND I PLEDGE ON MY LIFE THAT YOU WILL GO NO FARTHER.
How very dramatic.

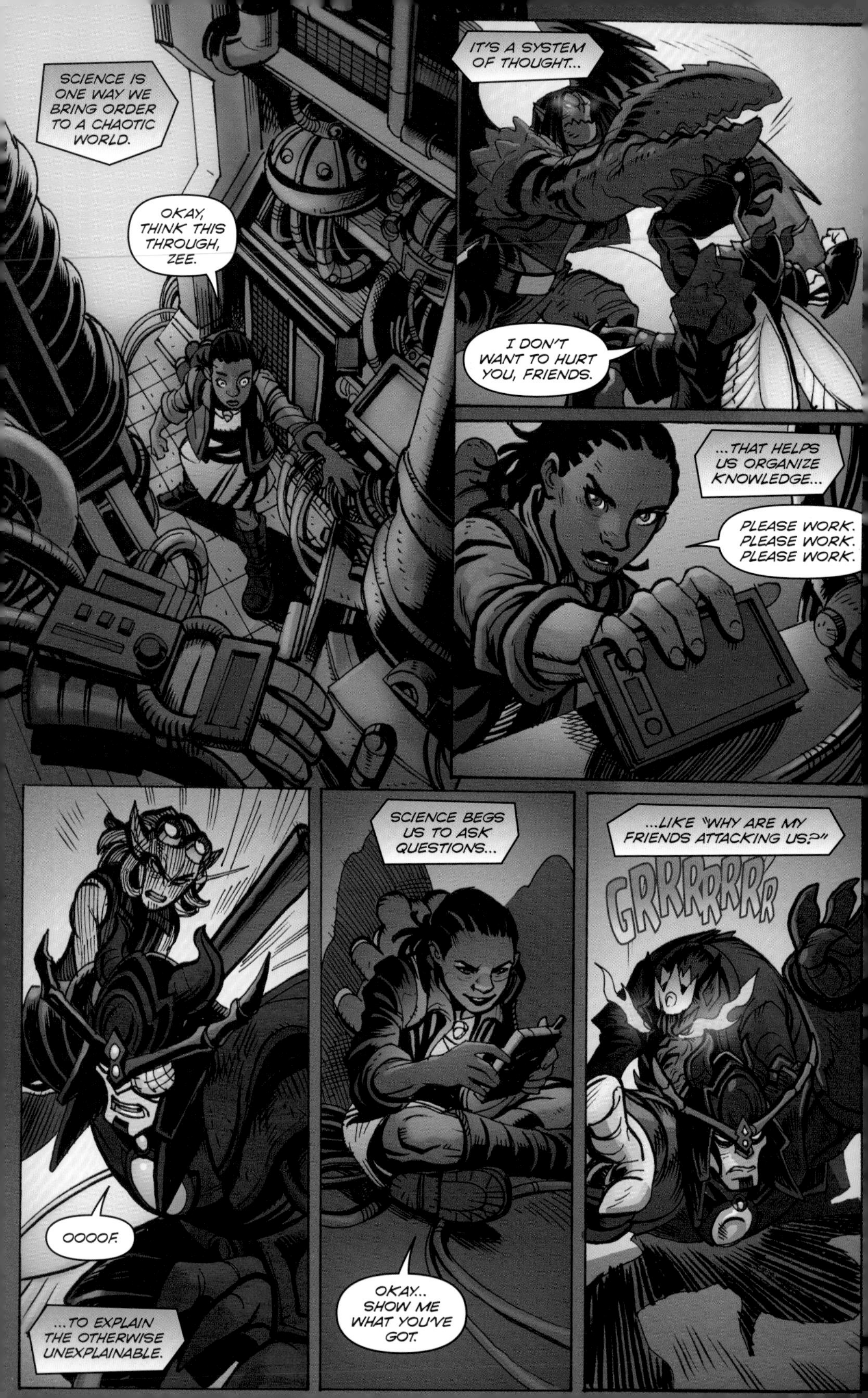
SCIENCE IS ONE WAY WE BRING ORDER TO A CHAOTIC WORLD.
OKAY, THINK THIS THROUGH, ZEE.
IT'S A SYSTEM OF THOUGHT...
I DON'T WANT TO HURT YOU, FRIENDS.
...THAT HELPS US ORGANIZE KNOWLEDGE...
PLEASE WORK. PLEASE WORK. PLEASE WORK.
OOOOF.
...TO EXPLAIN THE OTHERWISE UNEXPLAINABLE.
SCIENCE BEGS US TO ASK QUESTIONS...
OKAY... SHOW ME WHAT YOU'VE GOT.
...LIKE "WHY ARE MY FRIENDS ATTACKING US?"
GRRRRRRR

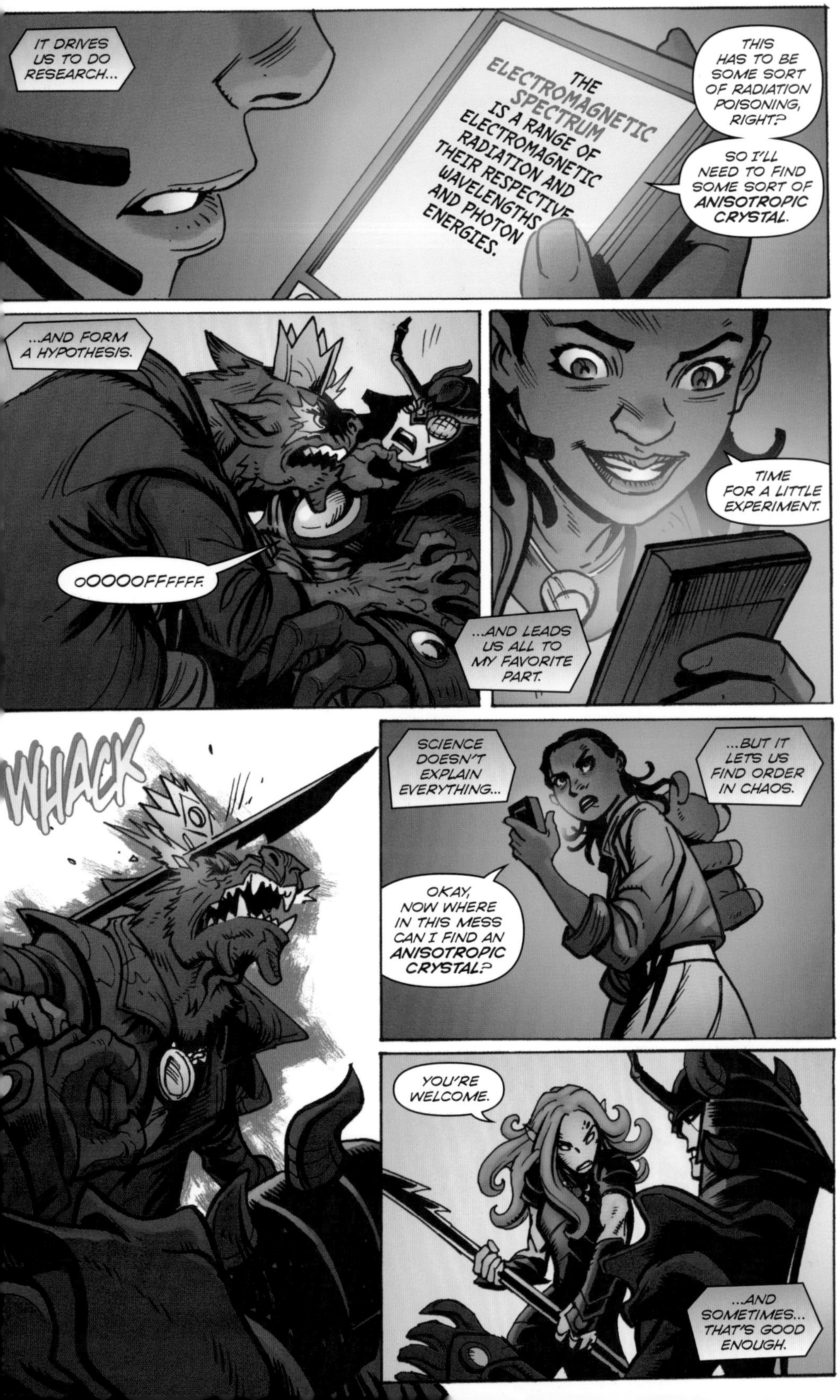
IT DRIVES US TO DO RESEARCH...
THE ELECTROMAGNETIC SPECTRUM IS A RANGE OF ELECTROMAGNETIC RADIATION AND THEIR RESPECTIVE WAVELENGTHS AND PHOTON ENERGIES.
THIS HAS TO BE SOME SORT OF RADIATION POISONING, RIGHT?
SO I'LL NEED TO FIND SOME SORT OF ANISOTROPIC CRYSTAL.
...AND FORM A HYPOTHESIS.
OOOOOFFFFFF.
TIME FOR A LITTLE EXPERIMENT.
...AND LEADS US ALL TO MY FAVORITE PART.
WHACK
SCIENCE DOESN'T EXPLAIN EVERYTHING...
...BUT IT LETS US FIND ORDER IN CHAOS.
OKAY, NOW WHERE IN THIS MESS CAN I FIND AN ANISOTROPIC CRYSTAL?
YOU'RE WELCOME.
...AND SOMETIMES... THAT'S GOOD ENOUGH.

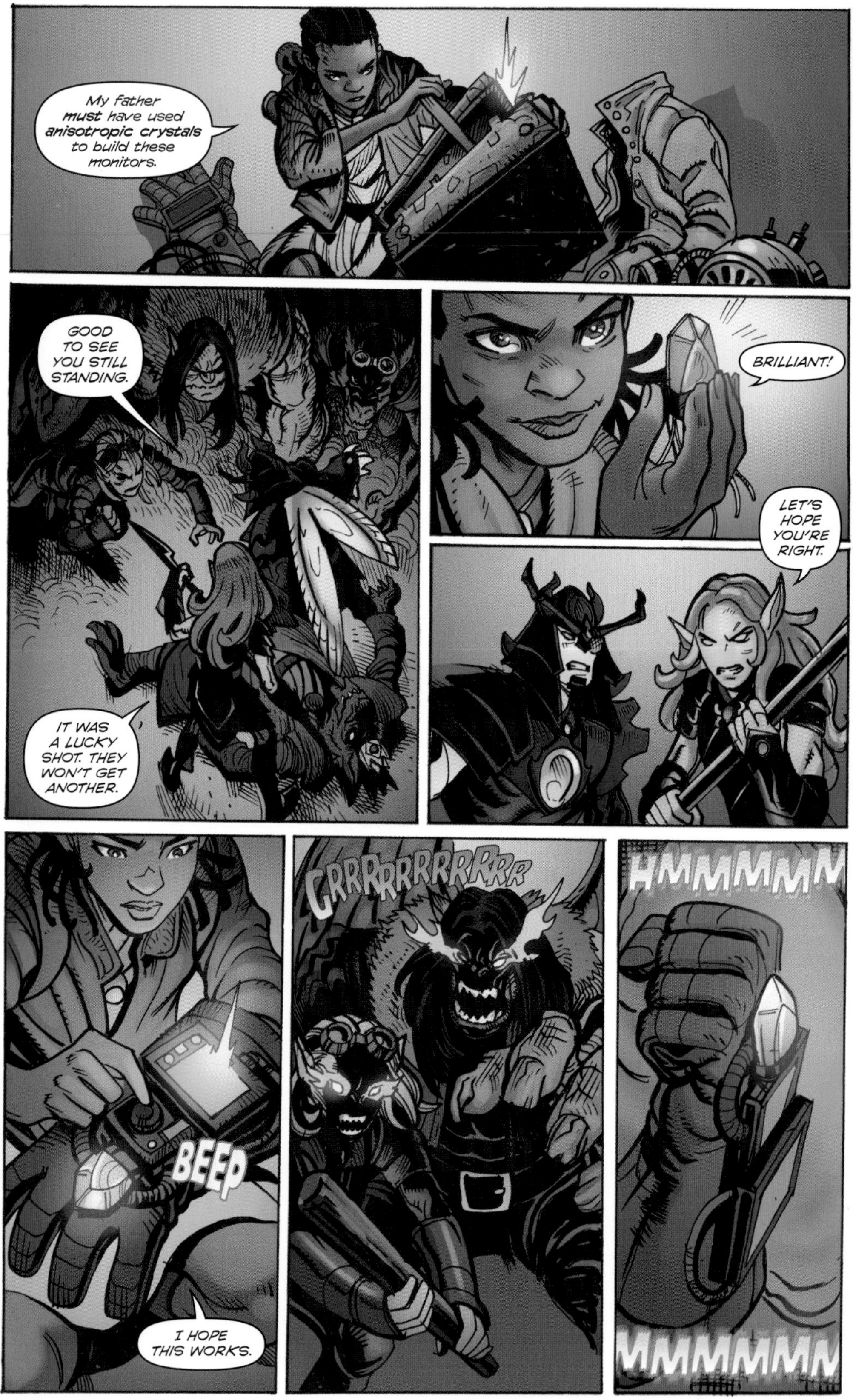
My father must have used anisotropic crystals to build these monitors.
GOOD TO SEE YOU STILL STANDING.
IT WAS A LUCKY SHOT. THEY WON'T GET ANOTHER.
BRILLIANT!
LET'S HOPE YOU'RE RIGHT.
BEEP
I HOPE THIS WORKS.
GRRRRRRRRRRR
HMMMMMN
MMMMMMN

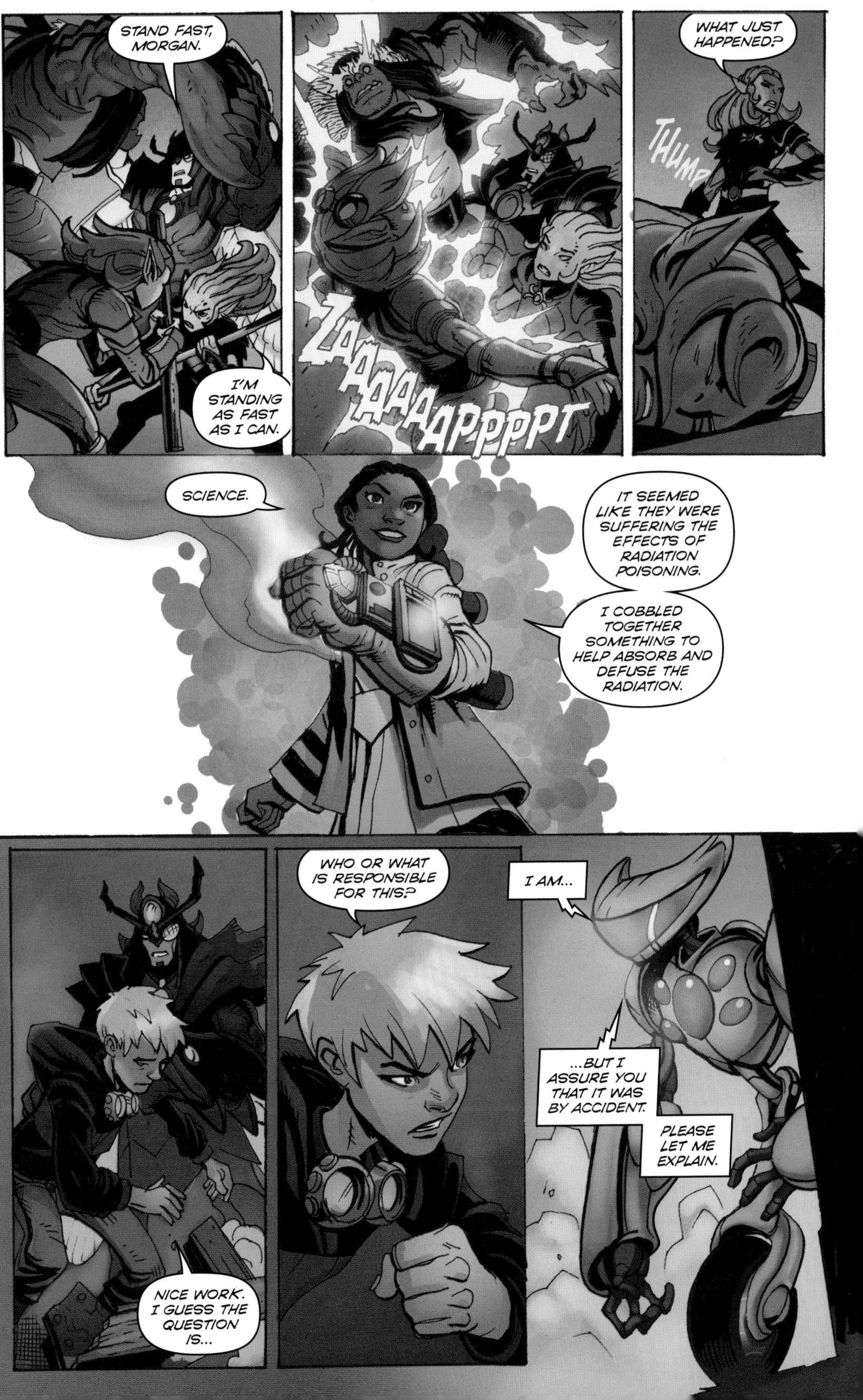
STAND FAST, MORGAN.
I'M STANDING AS FAST AS I CAN.
ZAAAAAAPPPPPT
WHAT JUST HAPPENED?
THUMP
SCIENCE.
IT SEEMED LIKE THEY WERE SUFFERING THE EFFECTS OF RADIATION POISONING.
I COBBLED TOGETHER SOMETHING TO HELP ABSORB AND DEFUSE THE RADIATION.
NICE WORK. I GUESS THE QUESTION IS...
WHO OR WHAT IS RESPONSIBLE FOR THIS?
I AM...
...BUT I ASSURE YOU THAT IT WAS BY ACCIDENT.
PLEASE LET ME EXPLAIN.

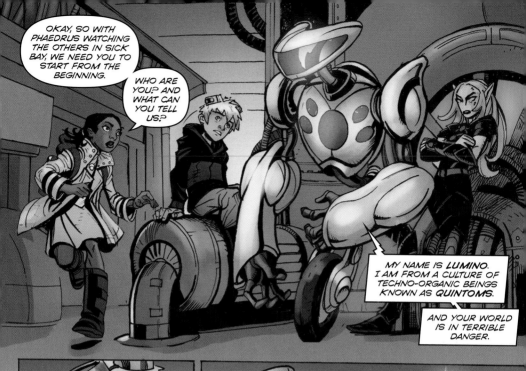

OKAY, SO WITH PHAEDRUS WATCHING THE OTHERS IN SICK BAY, WE NEED YOU TO START FROM THE BEGINNING.

WHO ARE YOU? AND WHAT CAN YOU TELL US?

MY NAME IS *LUMINO*. I AM FROM A CULTURE OF TECHNO-ORGANIC BEINGS KNOWN AS *QUINTOMS*.

AND YOUR WORLD IS IN TERRIBLE DANGER.

OUR WORLD IS *ALWAYS* IN TERRIBLE DANGER. WHAT'S NEW?

THE CONSORTIUM, A CABAL OF ROGUE SCIENTISTS, RECENTLY DISCOVERED THE *AFTERALL*.

AFTERALL? THEA AND I ONCE ENCOUNTERED FOES POSSESSED BY ITS ENERGY.

IT'S A PRIMAL FORCE OF THE UNIVERSE, YES?

CORRECT. IMAGINE THE UNIVERSE. NOW IMAGINE EVERYTHING BEYOND IT. THE AFTERALL HAS THE POWER TO RESHAPE TIME, SPACE AND ALL OF REALITY.

... A PRIMAL FORCE OF THE UNIVERSE? WITH THE ABILITY TO RESHAPE TIME? SOUNDS LIKE SOMETHING MY FATHER WOULD HAVE WORKED ON.

ACCORDING TO MY RESEARCH, IT WAS ORIGINALLY DISCOVERED BY THIS HUMAN.

IT WAS THE BASIS FOR HIS TECHNOLOGY AND THE ENERGY THAT FORGED THIS PLANET.

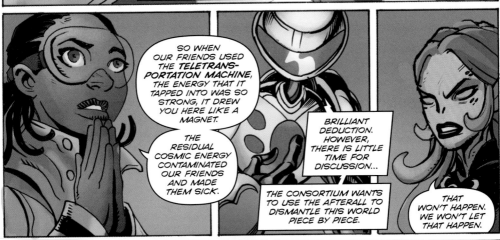

SO WHEN OUR FRIENDS USED THE **TELETRANS-PORTATION MACHINE,** THE ENERGY THAT IT TAPPED INTO WAS SO STRONG, IT DREW YOU HERE LIKE A MAGNET.

THE RESIDUAL COSMIC ENERGY CONTAMINATED OUR FRIENDS AND MADE THEM SICK.

BRILLIANT DEDUCTION. HOWEVER, THERE IS LITTLE TIME FOR DISCUSSION...

THE CONSORTIUM WANTS TO USE THE AFTERALL TO DISMANTLE THIS WORLD PIECE BY PIECE.

THAT WON'T HAPPEN. WE WON'T LET THAT HAPPEN.

THERE IS HOPE. BEYOND THESE SEAS OF INFINITY, THERE IS AN UNSEEN CITY. ONE THAT DOESN'T SHOW UP ON YOUR MAPS. THERE YOU WILL FIND THE PRIMORDIAL INTELLIGENCE KNOWN AS **TERRAN.**

IF THERE IS HOPE FOR YOUR WORLD, HE IS IT.

UNSEEN CITY? LIKE INVISIBLE? HOW ARE WE SUPPOSED TO FIND AN INVISIBLE CITY?

I THINK I KNOW...

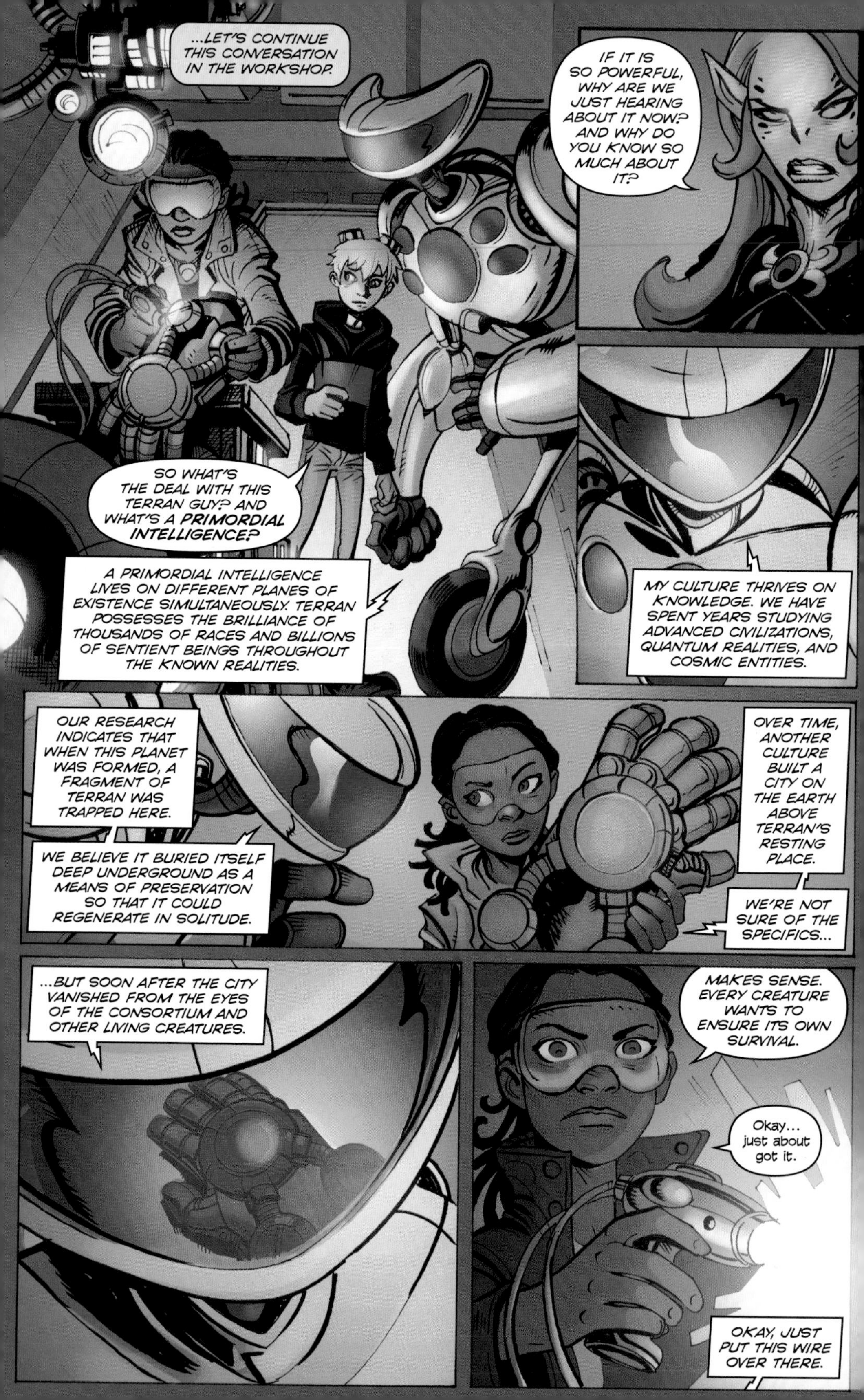
...LET'S CONTINUE THIS CONVERSATION IN THE WORKSHOP.
IF IT IS SO POWERFUL, WHY ARE WE JUST HEARING ABOUT IT NOW? AND WHY DO YOU KNOW SO MUCH ABOUT IT?
SO WHAT'S THE DEAL WITH THIS TERRAN GUY? AND WHAT'S A PRIMORDIAL INTELLIGENCE?
A PRIMORDIAL INTELLIGENCE LIVES ON DIFFERENT PLANES OF EXISTENCE SIMULTANEOUSLY. TERRAN POSSESSES THE BRILLIANCE OF THOUSANDS OF RACES AND BILLIONS OF SENTIENT BEINGS THROUGHOUT THE KNOWN REALITIES.
MY CULTURE THRIVES ON KNOWLEDGE. WE HAVE SPENT YEARS STUDYING ADVANCED CIVILIZATIONS, QUANTUM REALITIES, AND COSMIC ENTITIES.
OUR RESEARCH INDICATES THAT WHEN THIS PLANET WAS FORMED, A FRAGMENT OF TERRAN WAS TRAPPED HERE.
WE BELIEVE IT BURIED ITSELF DEEP UNDERGROUND AS A MEANS OF PRESERVATION SO THAT IT COULD REGENERATE IN SOLITUDE.
OVER TIME, ANOTHER CULTURE BUILT A CITY ON THE EARTH ABOVE TERRAN'S RESTING PLACE.
WE'RE NOT SURE OF THE SPECIFICS...
...BUT SOON AFTER THE CITY VANISHED FROM THE EYES OF THE CONSORTIUM AND OTHER LIVING CREATURES.
MAKES SENSE. EVERY CREATURE WANTS TO ENSURE ITS OWN SURVIVAL.
Okay... just about got it.
OKAY, JUST PUT THIS WIRE OVER THERE.

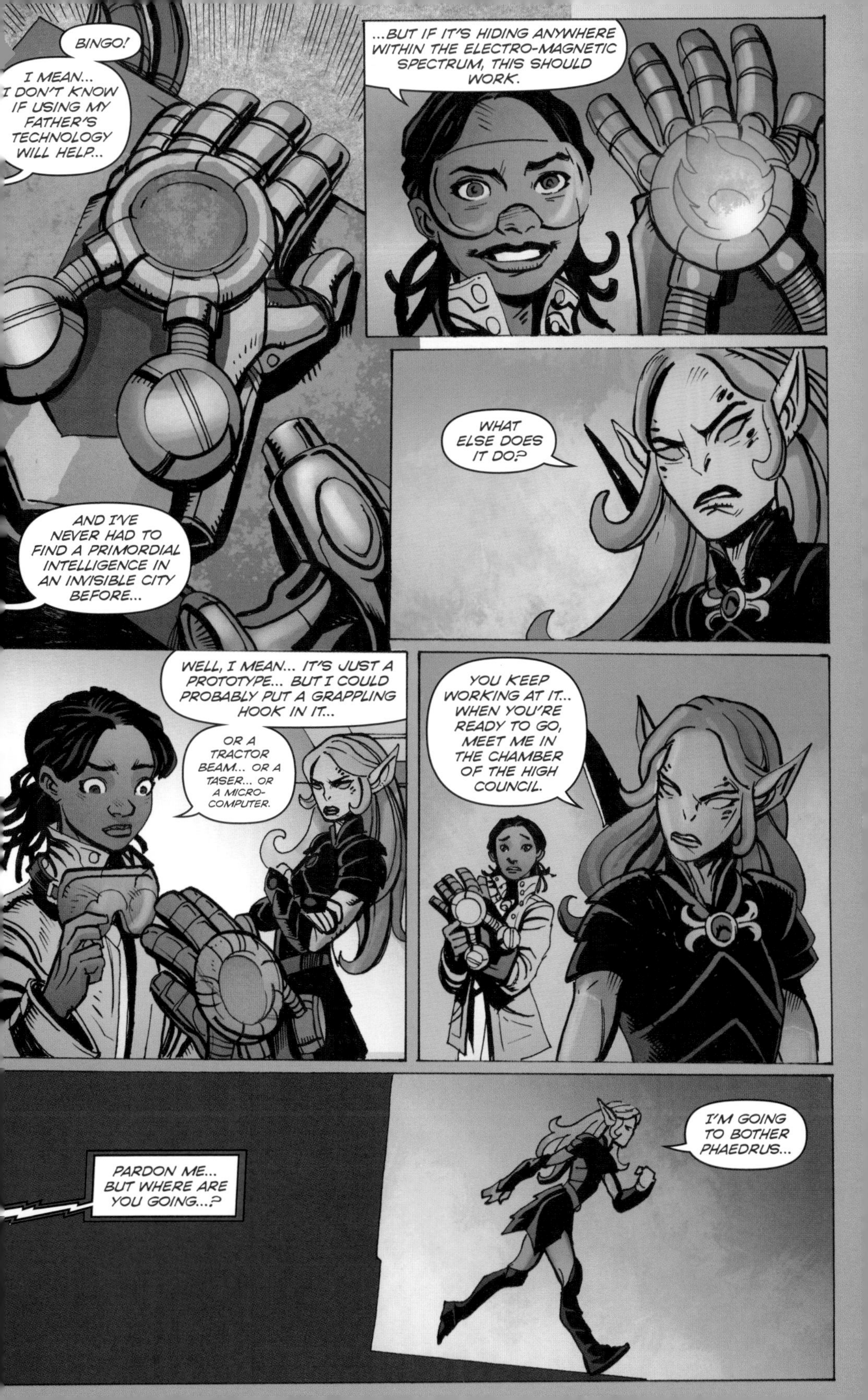
BINGO!
I MEAN... I DON'T KNOW IF USING MY FATHER'S TECHNOLOGY WILL HELP...
...BUT IF IT'S HIDING ANYWHERE WITHIN THE ELECTRO-MAGNETIC SPECTRUM, THIS SHOULD WORK.
AND I'VE NEVER HAD TO FIND A PRIMORDIAL INTELLIGENCE IN AN INVISIBLE CITY BEFORE...
WHAT ELSE DOES IT DO?
WELL, I MEAN... IT'S JUST A PROTOTYPE... BUT I COULD PROBABLY PUT A GRAPPLING HOOK IN IT...
OR A TRACTOR BEAM... OR A TASER... OR A MICRO-COMPUTER.
YOU KEEP WORKING AT IT... WHEN YOU'RE READY TO GO, MEET ME IN THE CHAMBER OF THE HIGH COUNCIL.
PARDON ME... BUT WHERE ARE YOU GOING...?
I'M GOING TO BOTHER PHAEDRUS...

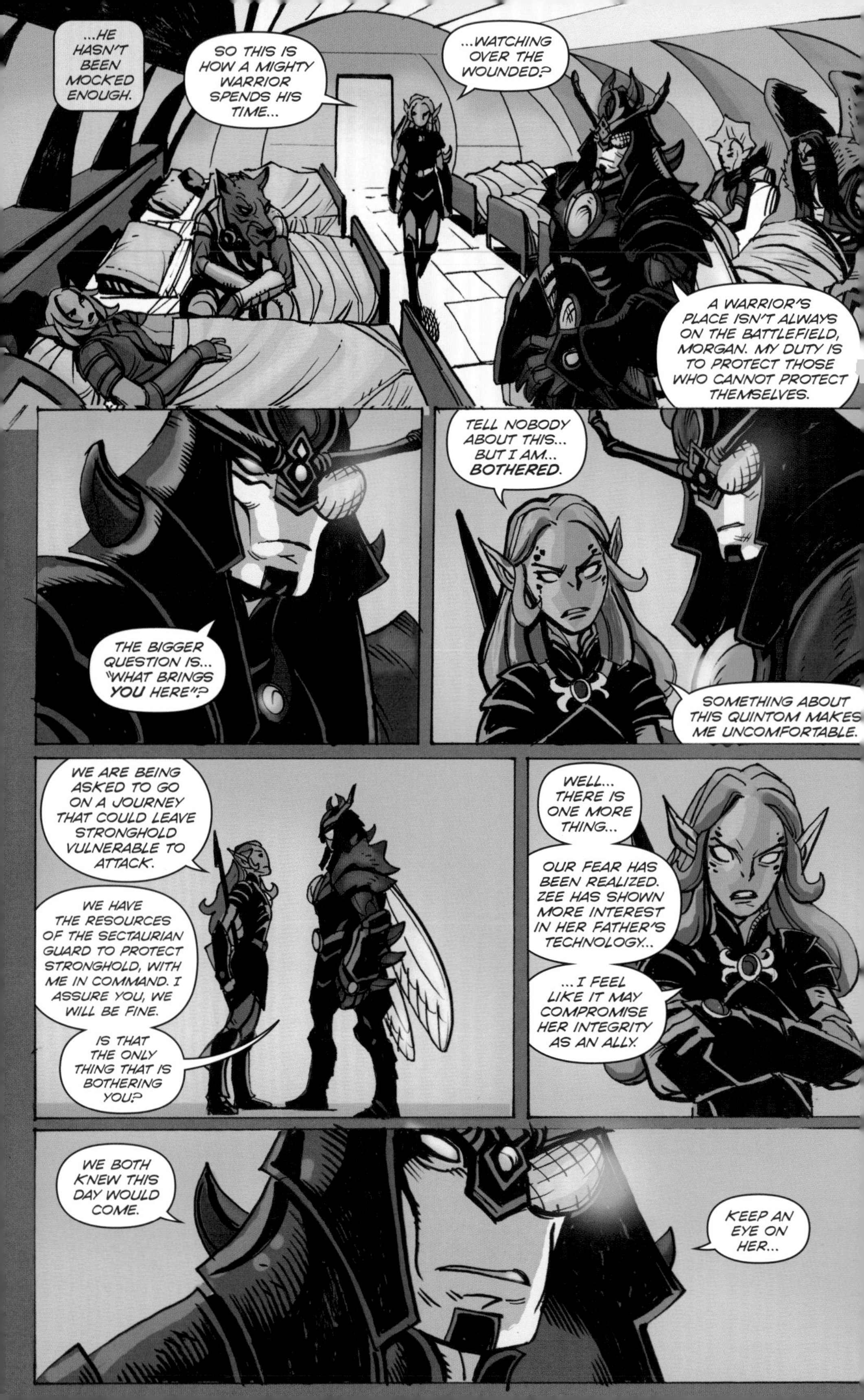

...HE HASN'T BEEN MOCKED ENOUGH.
SO THIS IS HOW A MIGHTY WARRIOR SPENDS HIS TIME...
...WATCHING OVER THE WOUNDED?
A WARRIOR'S PLACE ISN'T ALWAYS ON THE BATTLEFIELD, MORGAN. MY DUTY IS TO PROTECT THOSE WHO CANNOT PROTECT THEMSELVES.
THE BIGGER QUESTION IS... "WHAT BRINGS YOU HERE"?
TELL NOBODY ABOUT THIS... BUT I AM... BOTHERED.
SOMETHING ABOUT THIS QUINTOM MAKES ME UNCOMFORTABLE.
WE ARE BEING ASKED TO GO ON A JOURNEY THAT COULD LEAVE STRONGHOLD VULNERABLE TO ATTACK.
WE HAVE THE RESOURCES OF THE SECTAURIAN GUARD TO PROTECT STRONGHOLD, WITH ME IN COMMAND. I ASSURE YOU, WE WILL BE FINE.
IS THAT THE ONLY THING THAT IS BOTHERING YOU?
WELL... THERE IS ONE MORE THING...
OUR FEAR HAS BEEN REALIZED. ZEE HAS SHOWN MORE INTEREST IN HER FATHER'S TECHNOLOGY...
...I FEEL LIKE IT MAY COMPROMISE HER INTEGRITY AS AN ALLY.
WE BOTH KNEW THIS DAY WOULD COME.
KEEP AN EYE ON HER...

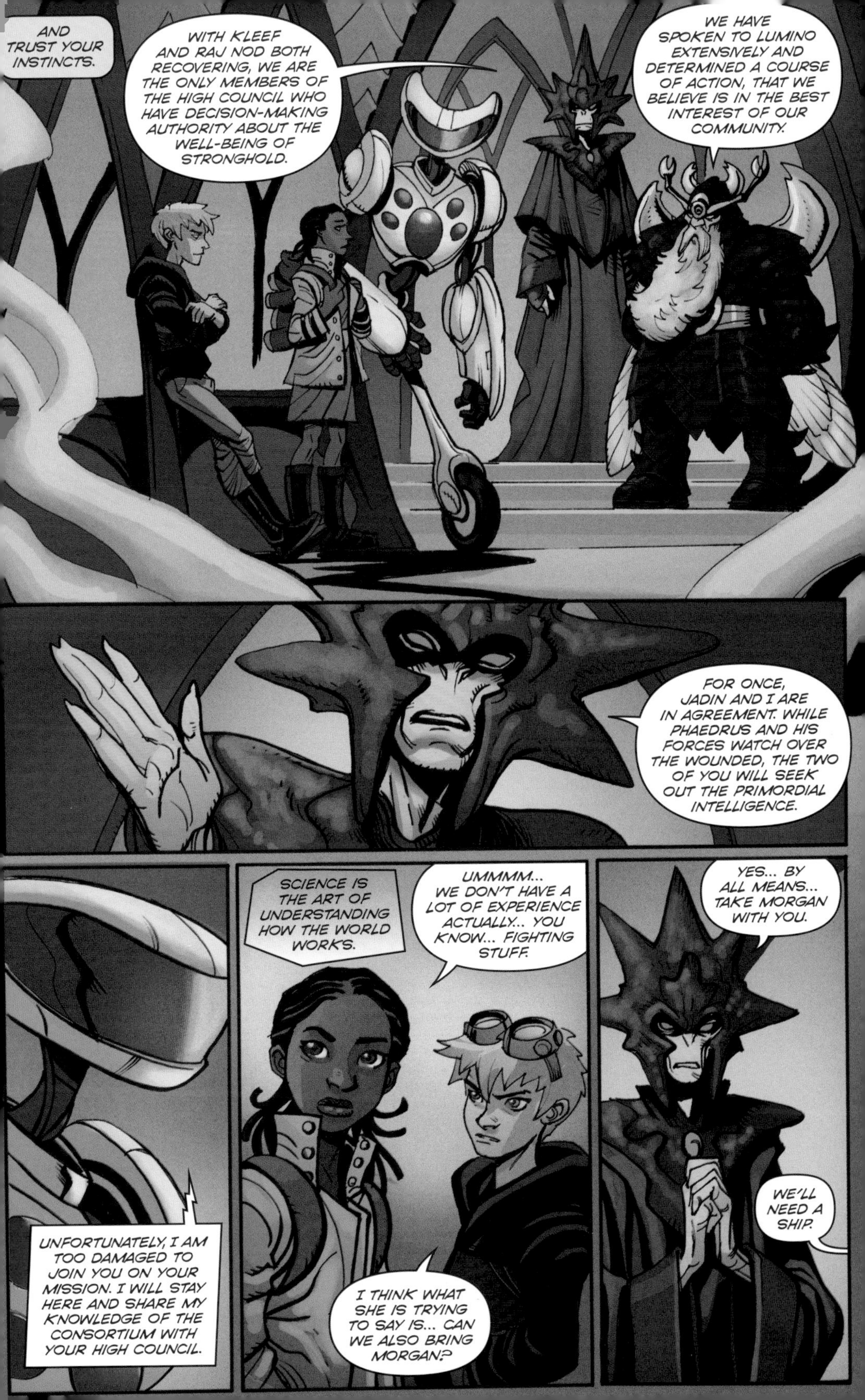
AND TRUST YOUR INSTINCTS.
WITH KLEEF AND RAJ NOD BOTH RECOVERING, WE ARE THE ONLY MEMBERS OF THE HIGH COUNCIL WHO HAVE DECISION-MAKING AUTHORITY ABOUT THE WELL-BEING OF STRONGHOLD.
WE HAVE SPOKEN TO LUMINO EXTENSIVELY AND DETERMINED A COURSE OF ACTION, THAT WE BELIEVE IS IN THE BEST INTEREST OF OUR COMMUNITY.
FOR ONCE, JADIN AND I ARE IN AGREEMENT. WHILE PHAEDRUS AND HIS FORCES WATCH OVER THE WOUNDED, THE TWO OF YOU WILL SEEK OUT THE PRIMORDIAL INTELLIGENCE.
UNFORTUNATELY, I AM TOO DAMAGED TO JOIN YOU ON YOUR MISSION. I WILL STAY HERE AND SHARE MY KNOWLEDGE OF THE CONSORTIUM WITH YOUR HIGH COUNCIL.
SCIENCE IS THE ART OF UNDERSTANDING HOW THE WORLD WORKS.
UMMMM... WE DON'T HAVE A LOT OF EXPERIENCE ACTUALLY... YOU KNOW... FIGHTING STUFF.
I THINK WHAT SHE IS TRYING TO SAY IS... CAN WE ALSO BRING MORGAN?
YES... BY ALL MEANS... TAKE MORGAN WITH YOU.
WE'LL NEED A SHIP.

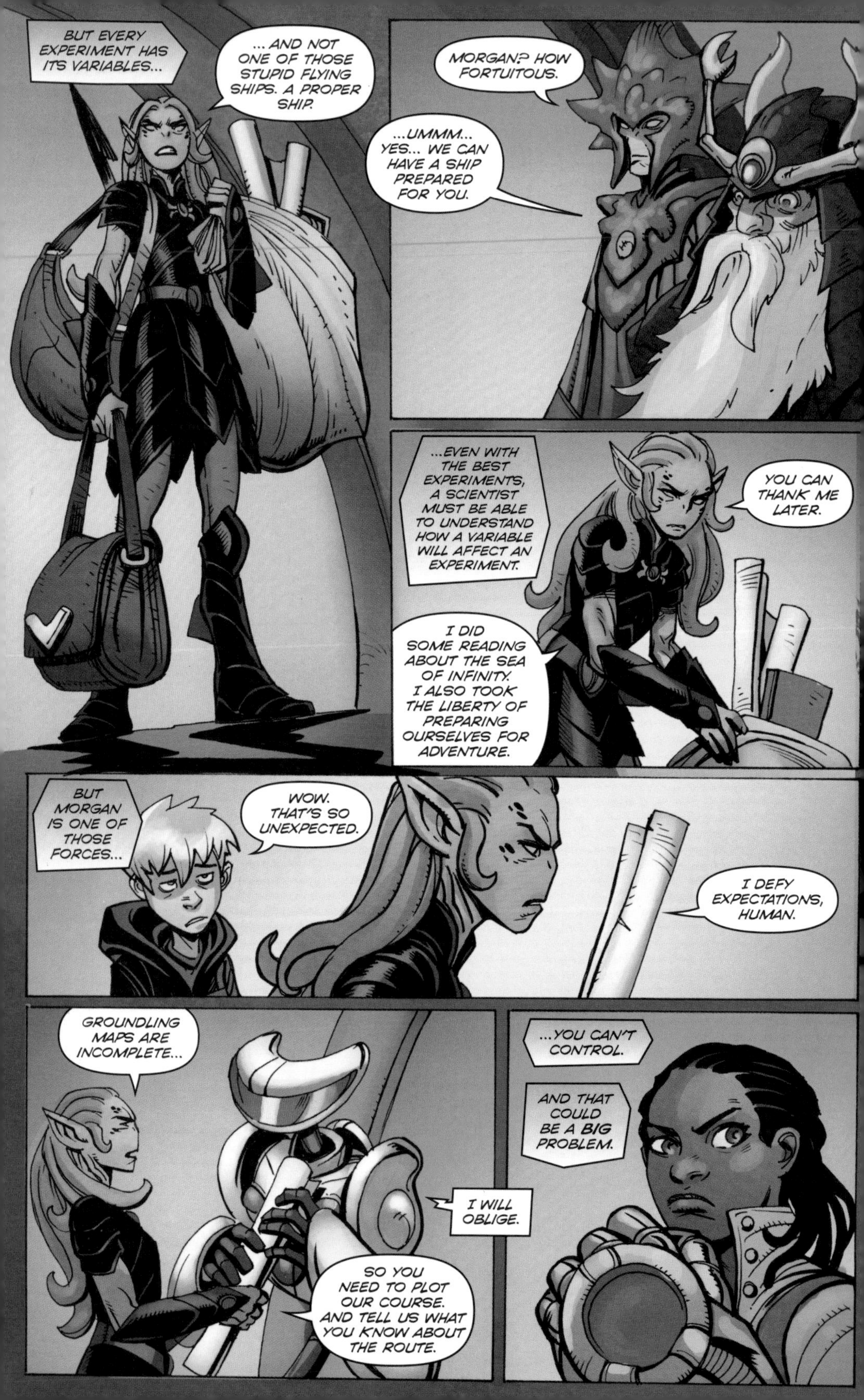
BUT EVERY EXPERIMENT HAS ITS VARIABLES...
...AND NOT ONE OF THOSE STUPID FLYING SHIPS. A PROPER SHIP.
MORGAN? HOW FORTUITOUS.
...UMMM... YES... WE CAN HAVE A SHIP PREPARED FOR YOU.
...EVEN WITH THE BEST EXPERIMENTS, A SCIENTIST MUST BE ABLE TO UNDERSTAND HOW A VARIABLE WILL AFFECT AN EXPERIMENT.
YOU CAN THANK ME LATER.
I DID SOME READING ABOUT THE SEA OF INFINITY. I ALSO TOOK THE LIBERTY OF PREPARING OURSELVES FOR ADVENTURE.
BUT MORGAN IS ONE OF THOSE FORCES...
WOW. THAT'S SO UNEXPECTED.
I DEFY EXPECTATIONS, HUMAN.
GROUNDLING MAPS ARE INCOMPLETE...
I WILL OBLIGE.
SO YOU NEED TO PLOT OUR COURSE. AND TELL US WHAT YOU KNOW ABOUT THE ROUTE.
...YOU CAN'T CONTROL.
AND THAT COULD BE A BIG PROBLEM.

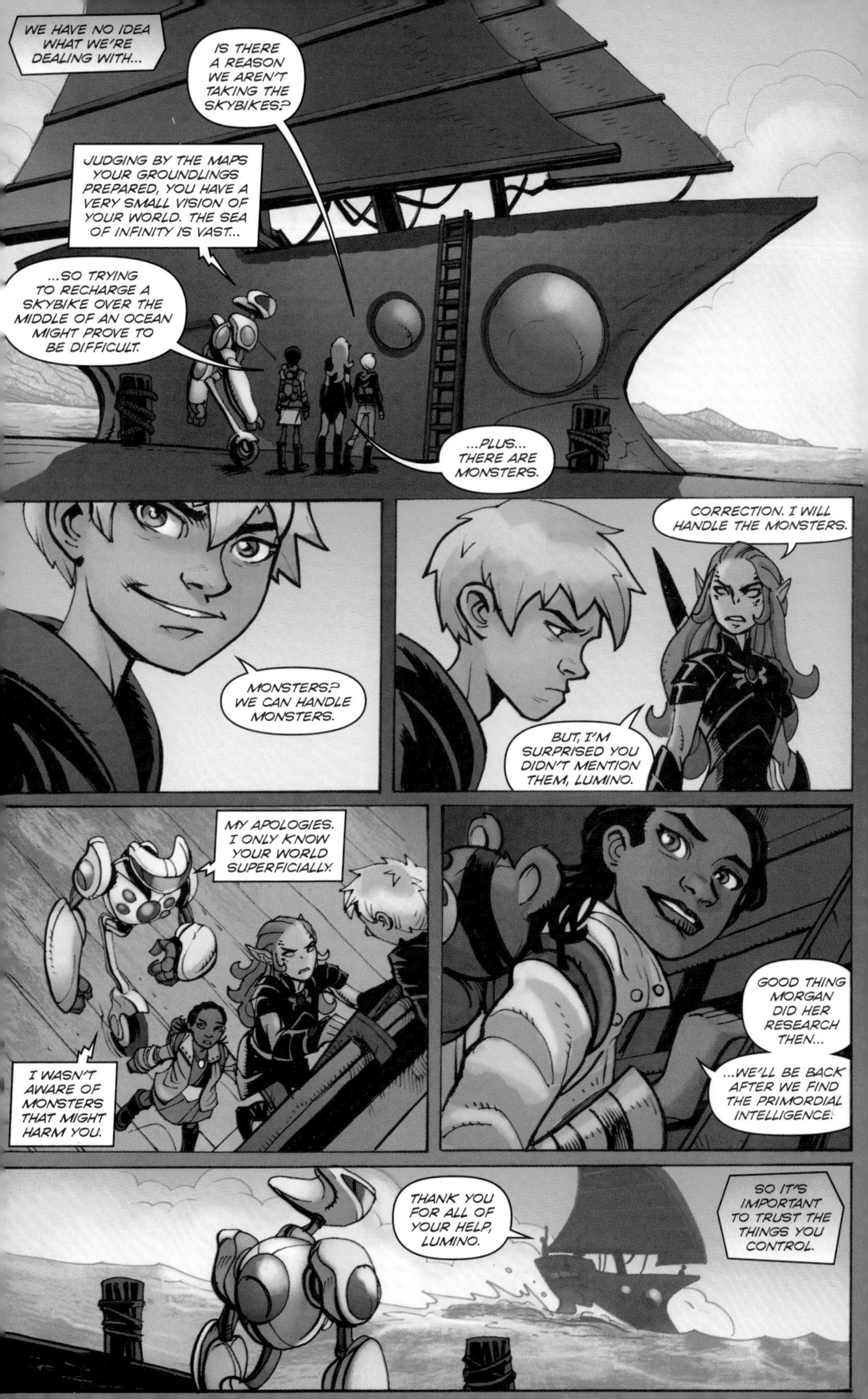
WE HAVE NO IDEA WHAT WE'RE DEALING WITH...
IS THERE A REASON WE AREN'T TAKING THE SKYBIKES?
JUDGING BY THE MAPS YOUR GROUNDLINGS PREPARED, YOU HAVE A VERY SMALL VISION OF YOUR WORLD. THE SEA OF INFINITY IS VAST...
...SO TRYING TO RECHARGE A SKYBIKE OVER THE MIDDLE OF AN OCEAN MIGHT PROVE TO BE DIFFICULT.
...PLUS... THERE ARE MONSTERS.
MONSTERS? WE CAN HANDLE MONSTERS.
CORRECTION. I WILL HANDLE THE MONSTERS.
BUT, I'M SURPRISED YOU DIDN'T MENTION THEM, LUMINO.
MY APOLOGIES. I ONLY KNOW YOUR WORLD SUPERFICIALLY.
I WASN'T AWARE OF MONSTERS THAT MIGHT HARM YOU.
GOOD THING MORGAN DID HER RESEARCH THEN...
...WE'LL BE BACK AFTER WE FIND THE PRIMORDIAL INTELLIGENCE.
THANK YOU FOR ALL OF YOUR HELP, LUMINO.
SO IT'S IMPORTANT TO TRUST THE THINGS YOU CONTROL.

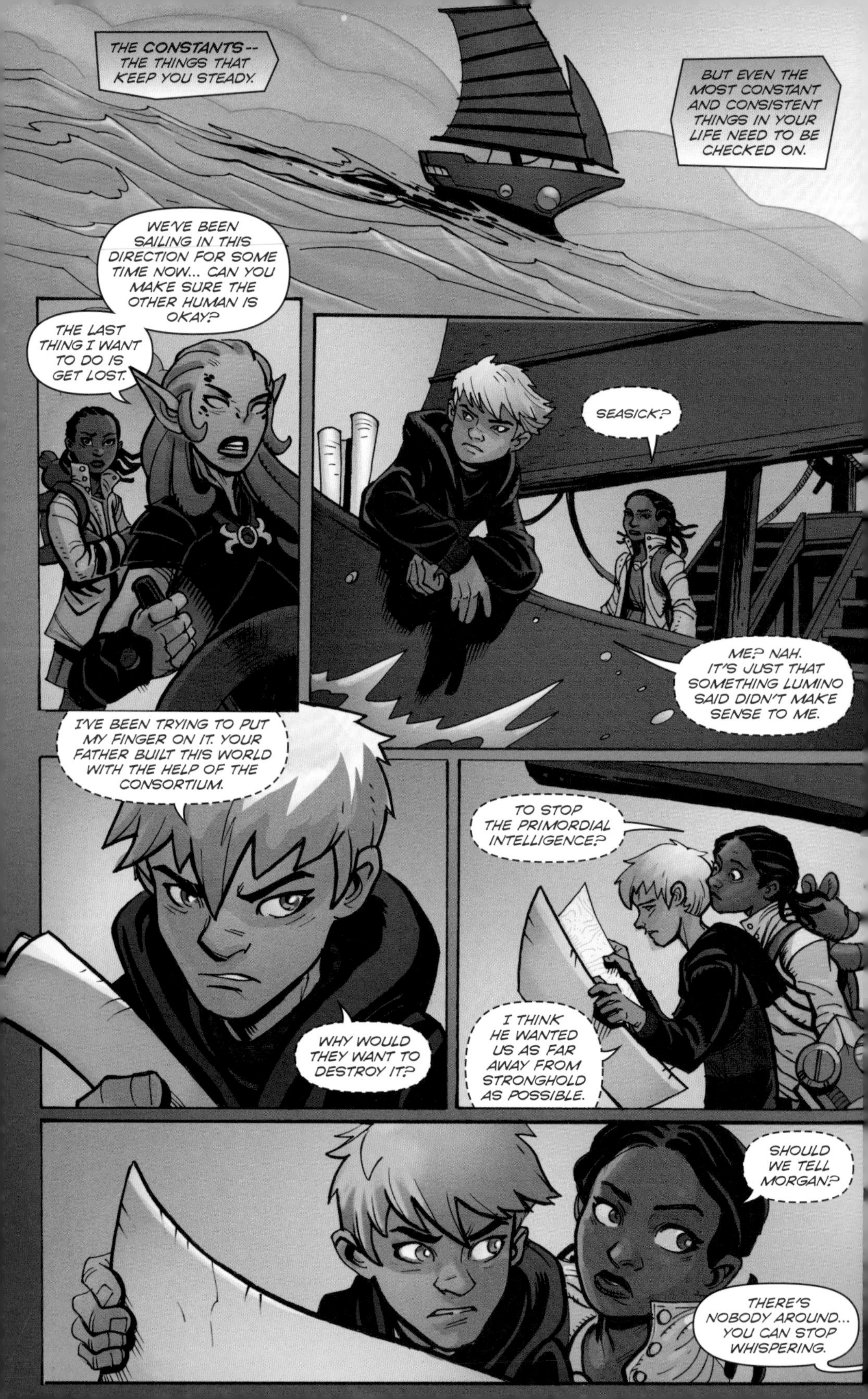
THE CONSTANTS-- THE THINGS THAT KEEP YOU STEADY.
BUT EVEN THE MOST CONSTANT AND CONSISTENT THINGS IN YOUR LIFE NEED TO BE CHECKED ON.
WE'VE BEEN SAILING IN THIS DIRECTION FOR SOME TIME NOW... CAN YOU MAKE SURE THE OTHER HUMAN IS OKAY?
THE LAST THING I WANT TO DO IS GET LOST.
SEASICK?
ME? NAH. IT'S JUST THAT SOMETHING LUMINO SAID DIDN'T MAKE SENSE TO ME.
I'VE BEEN TRYING TO PUT MY FINGER ON IT. YOUR FATHER BUILT THIS WORLD WITH THE HELP OF THE CONSORTIUM.
WHY WOULD THEY WANT TO DESTROY IT?
TO STOP THE PRIMORDIAL INTELLIGENCE?
I THINK HE WANTED US AS FAR AWAY FROM STRONGHOLD AS POSSIBLE.
SHOULD WE TELL MORGAN?
THERE'S NOBODY AROUND... YOU CAN STOP WHISPERING.

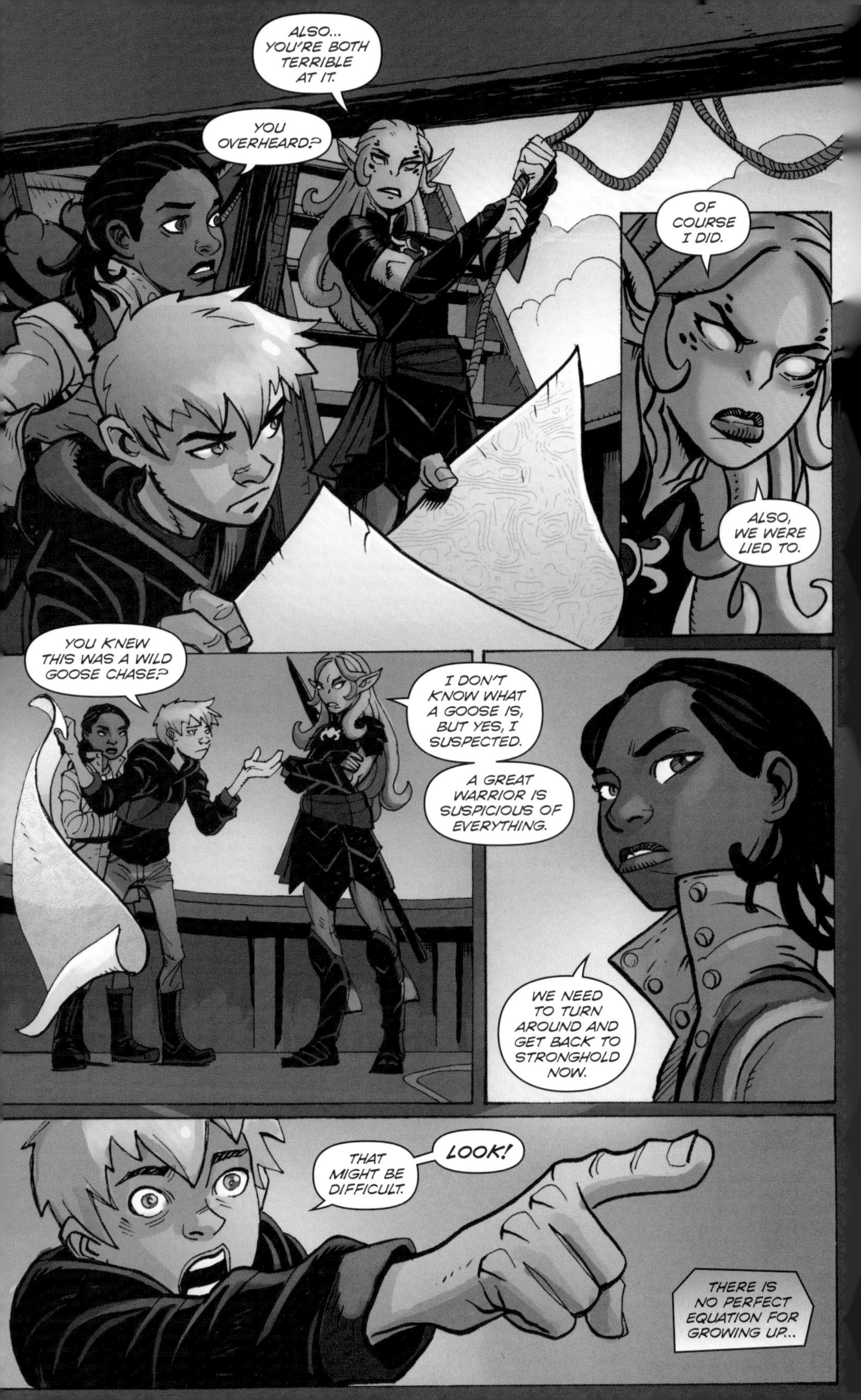

YOU OVERHEARD?
ALSO... YOU'RE BOTH TERRIBLE AT IT.
OF COURSE I DID.
ALSO, WE WERE LIED TO.
YOU KNEW THIS WAS A WILD GOOSE CHASE?
I DON'T KNOW WHAT A GOOSE IS, BUT YES, I SUSPECTED.
A GREAT WARRIOR IS SUSPICIOUS OF EVERYTHING.
WE NEED TO TURN AROUND AND GET BACK TO STRONGHOLD NOW.
THAT MIGHT BE DIFFICULT.
LOOK!
THERE IS NO PERFECT EQUATION FOR GROWING UP...

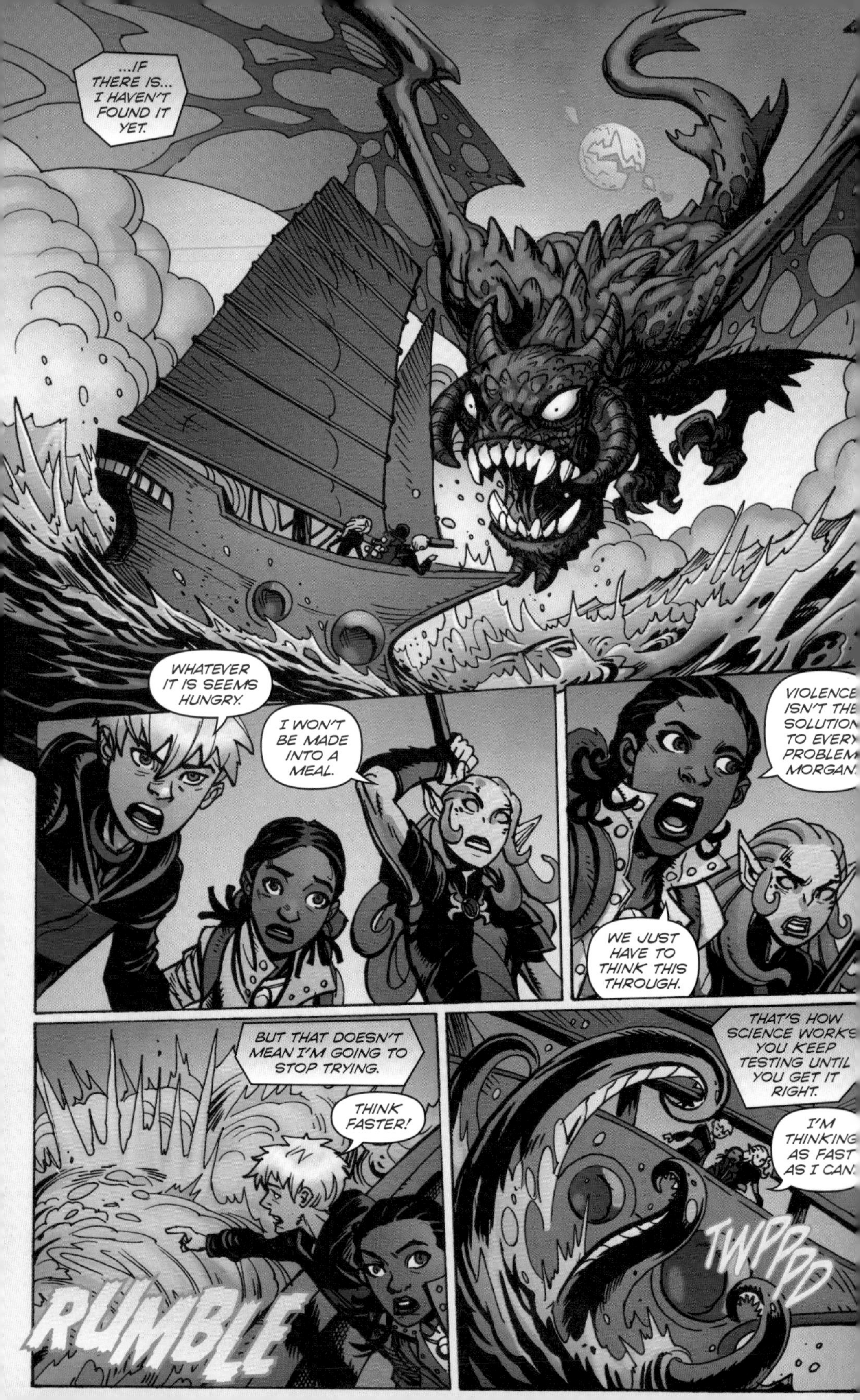
...IF THERE IS... I HAVEN'T FOUND IT YET.
WHATEVER IT IS SEEMS HUNGRY.
I WON'T BE MADE INTO A MEAL.
VIOLENCE ISN'T THE SOLUTION TO EVERY PROBLEM, MORGAN.
WE JUST HAVE TO THINK THIS THROUGH.
BUT THAT DOESN'T MEAN I'M GOING TO STOP TRYING.
THINK FASTER!
RUMBLE
THAT'S HOW SCIENCE WORKS. YOU KEEP TESTING UNTIL YOU GET IT RIGHT.
I'M THINKING AS FAST AS I CAN.
TWIPPPD

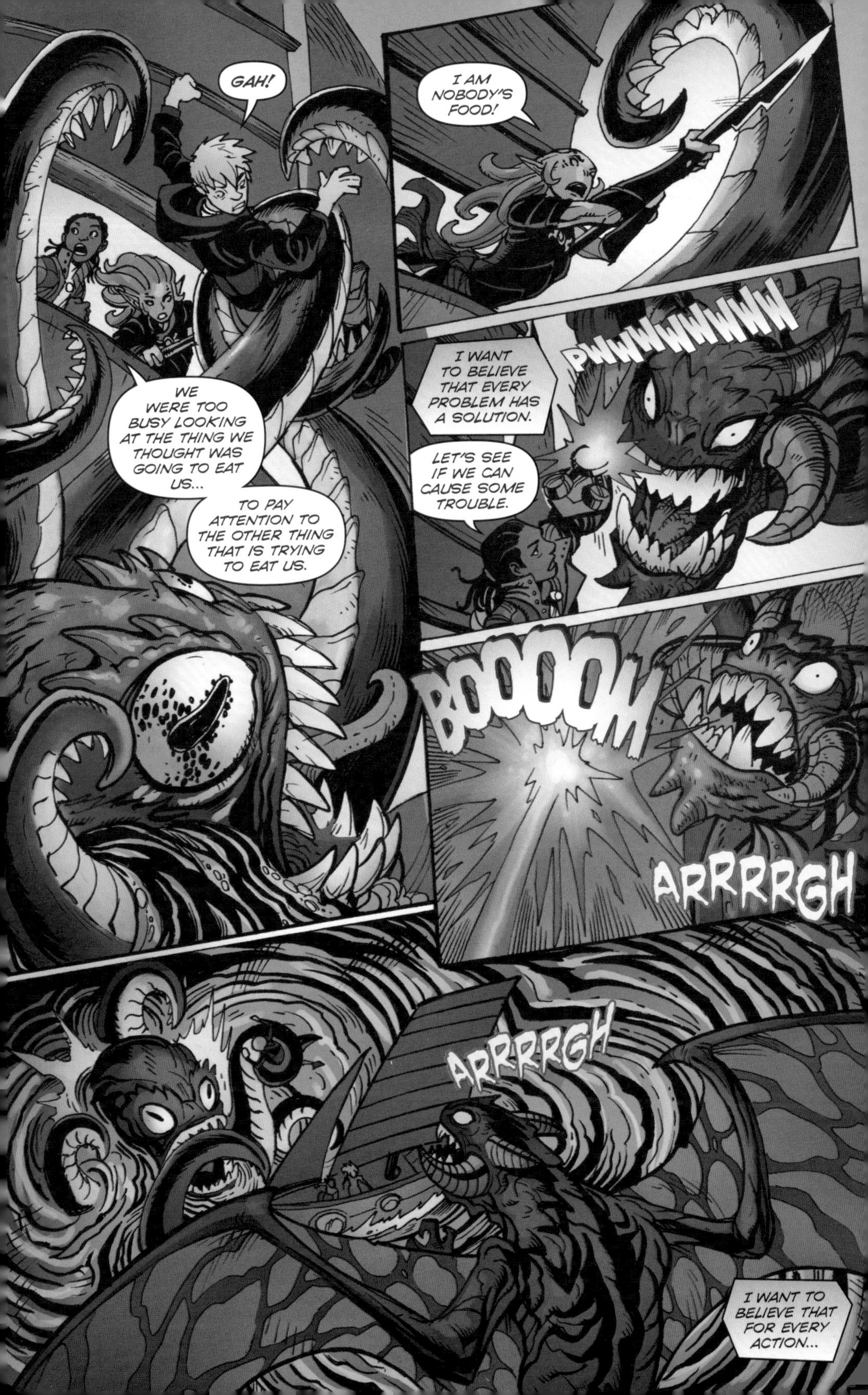
GAH!
WE WERE TOO BUSY LOOKING AT THE THING WE THOUGHT WAS GOING TO EAT US...
TO PAY ATTENTION TO THE OTHER THING THAT IS TRYING TO EAT US.
I AM NOBODY'S FOOD!
I WANT TO BELIEVE THAT EVERY PROBLEM HAS A SOLUTION.
LET'S SEE IF WE CAN CAUSE SOME TROUBLE.
PWWWWWWWW
BOOOOM
ARRRRGH
ARRRRGH
I WANT TO BELIEVE THAT FOR EVERY ACTION...

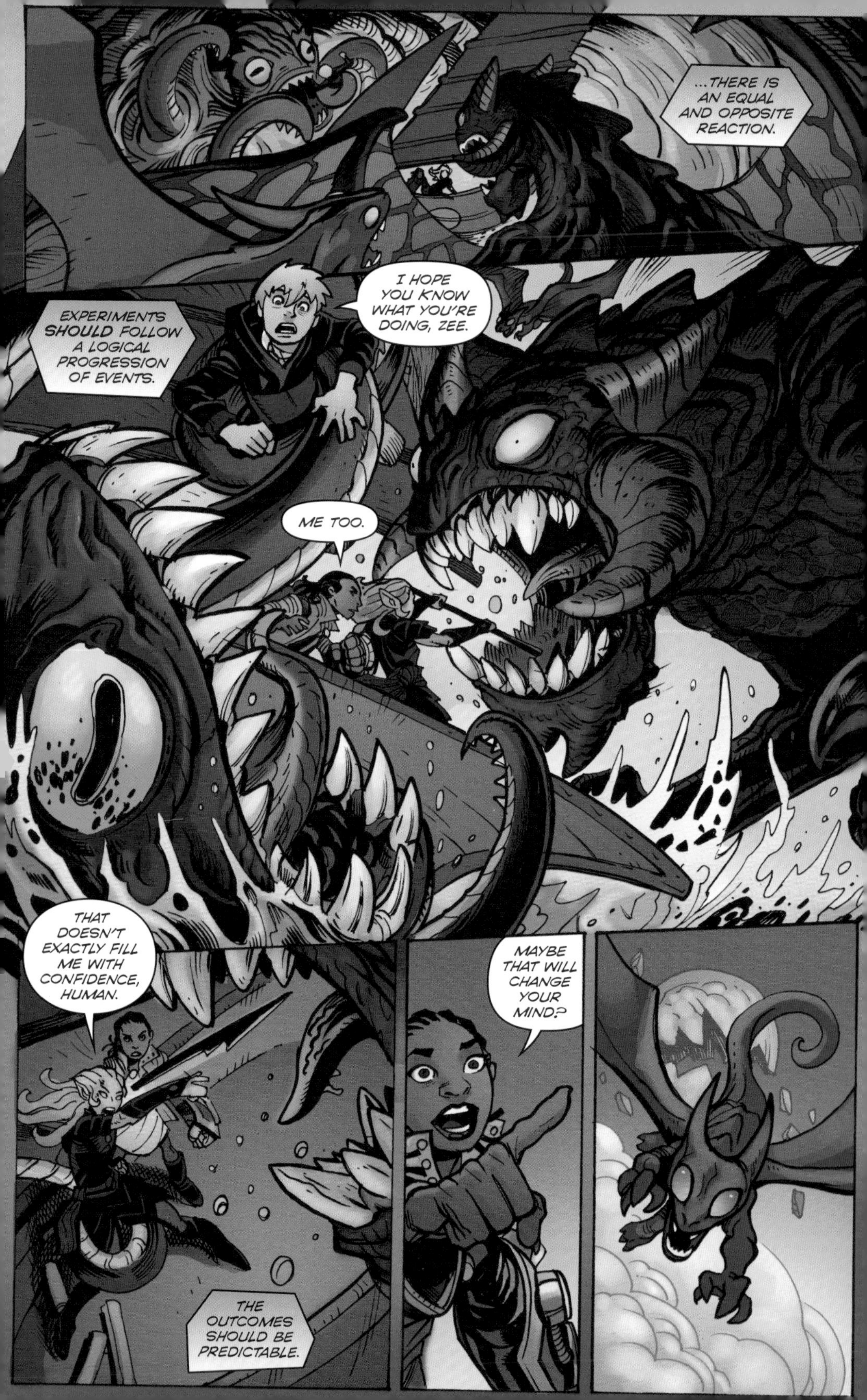
...THERE IS AN EQUAL AND OPPOSITE REACTION.
EXPERIMENTS SHOULD FOLLOW A LOGICAL PROGRESSION OF EVENTS.
I HOPE YOU KNOW WHAT YOU'RE DOING, ZEE.
ME TOO.
THAT DOESN'T EXACTLY FILL ME WITH CONFIDENCE, HUMAN.
THE OUTCOMES SHOULD BE PREDICTABLE.
MAYBE THAT WILL CHANGE YOUR MIND?

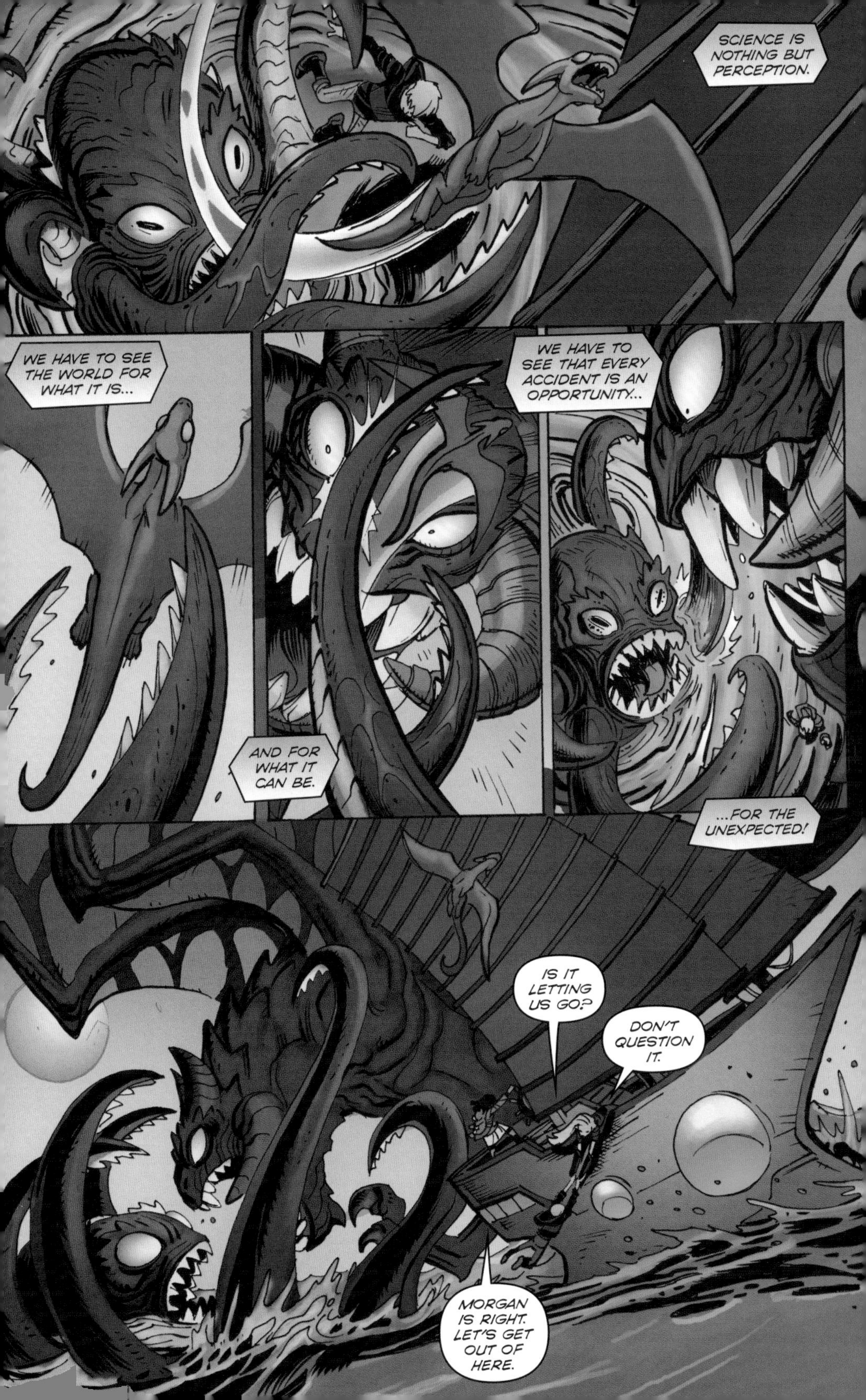
SCIENCE IS NOTHING BUT PERCEPTION.
WE HAVE TO SEE THE WORLD FOR WHAT IT IS...
AND FOR WHAT IT CAN BE.
WE HAVE TO SEE THAT EVERY ACCIDENT IS AN OPPORTUNITY...
...FOR THE UNEXPECTED!
IS IT LETTING US GO?
DON'T QUESTION IT.
MORGAN IS RIGHT. LET'S GET OUT OF HERE.

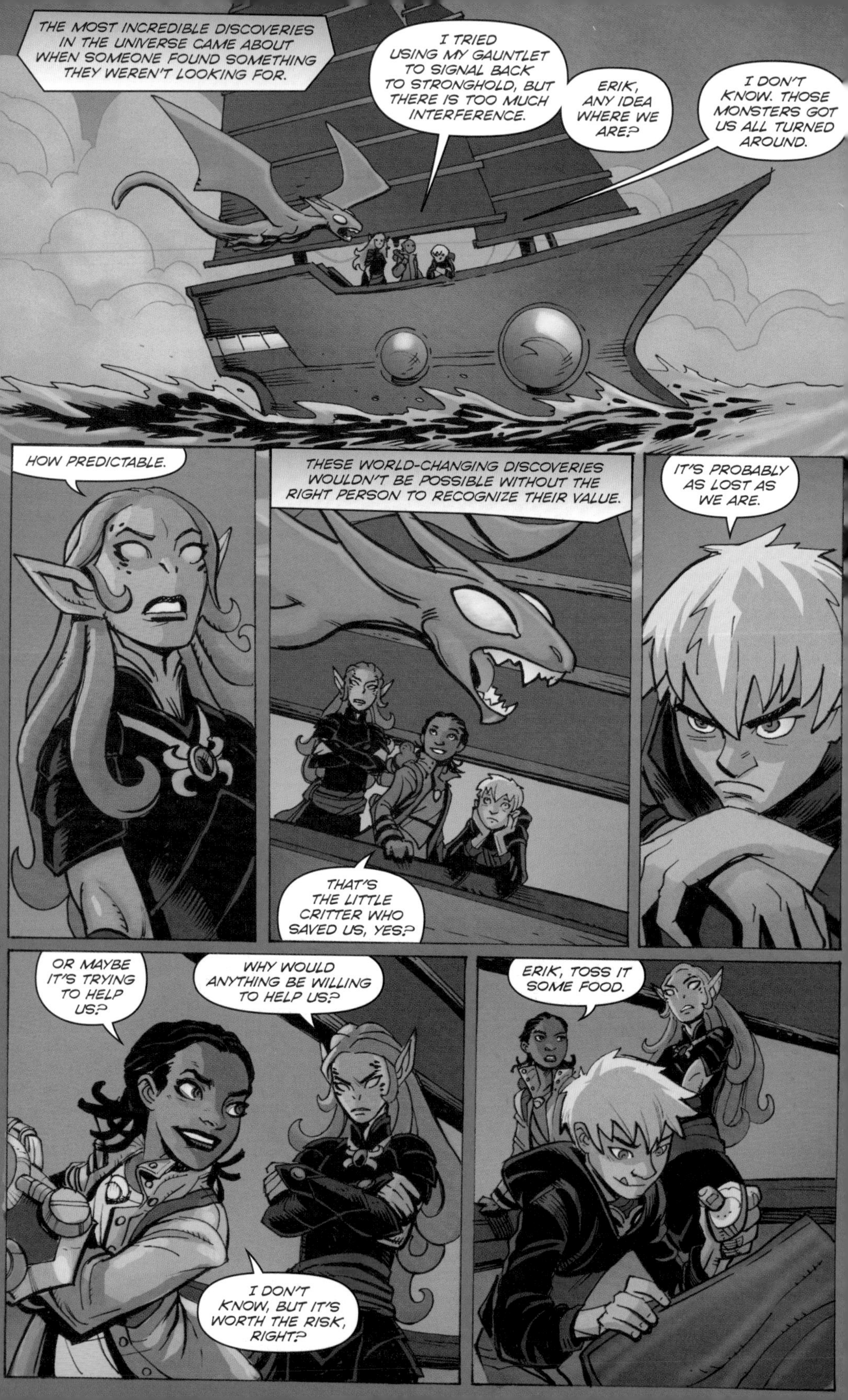
THE MOST INCREDIBLE DISCOVERIES IN THE UNIVERSE CAME ABOUT WHEN SOMEONE FOUND SOMETHING THEY WEREN'T LOOKING FOR.
I TRIED USING MY GAUNTLET TO SIGNAL BACK TO STRONGHOLD, BUT THERE IS TOO MUCH INTERFERENCE.
ERIK, ANY IDEA WHERE WE ARE?
I DON'T KNOW. THOSE MONSTERS GOT US ALL TURNED AROUND.
HOW PREDICTABLE.
THESE WORLD-CHANGING DISCOVERIES WOULDN'T BE POSSIBLE WITHOUT THE RIGHT PERSON TO RECOGNIZE THEIR VALUE.
THAT'S THE LITTLE CRITTER WHO SAVED US, YES?
IT'S PROBABLY AS LOST AS WE ARE.
OR MAYBE IT'S TRYING TO HELP US?
WHY WOULD ANYTHING BE WILLING TO HELP US?
I DON'T KNOW, BUT IT'S WORTH THE RISK, RIGHT?
ERIK, TOSS IT SOME FOOD.

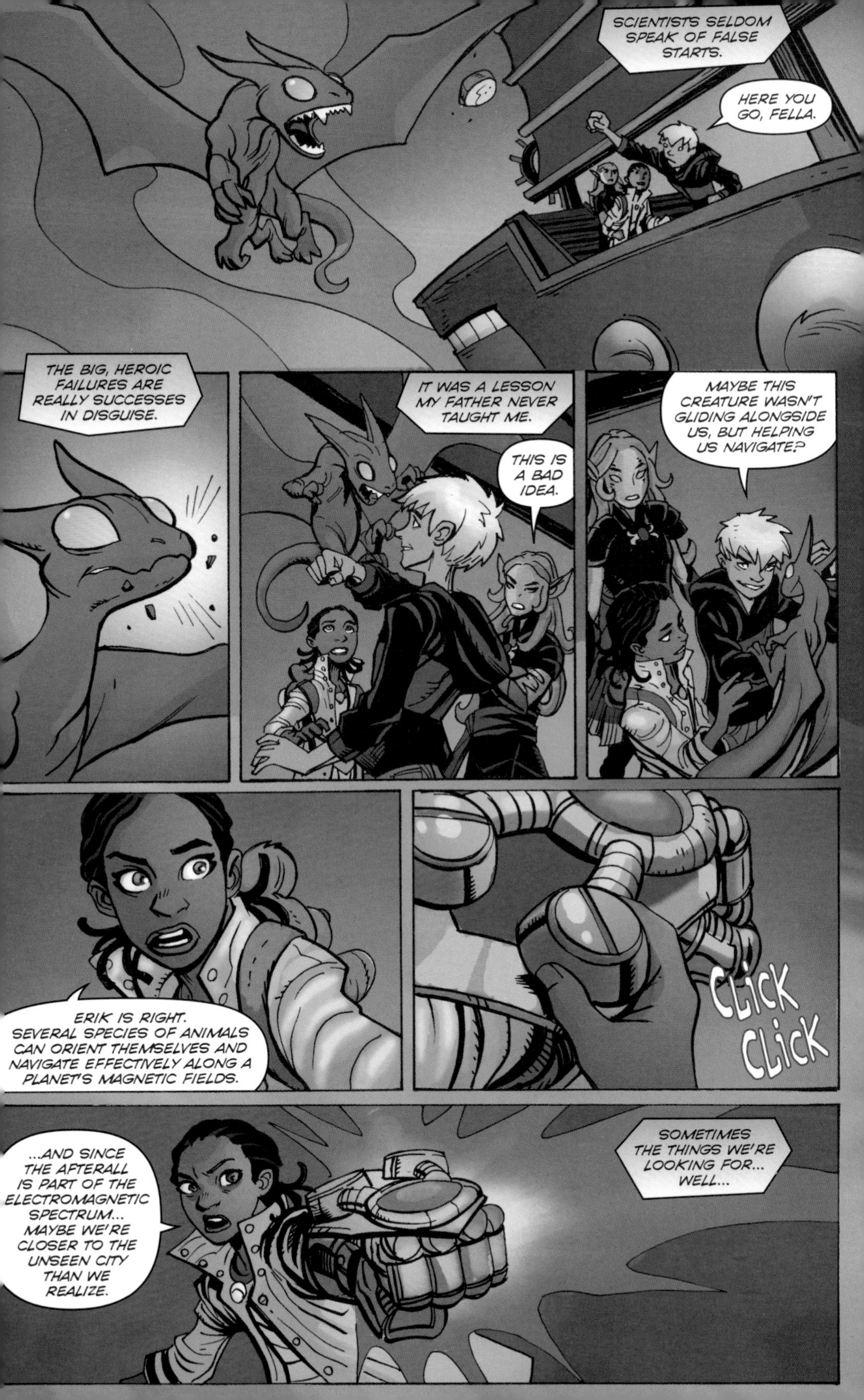
SCIENTISTS SELDOM SPEAK OF FALSE STARTS.
HERE YOU GO, FELLA.
THE BIG, HEROIC FAILURES ARE REALLY SUCCESSES IN DISGUISE.
IT WAS A LESSON MY FATHER NEVER TAUGHT ME.
THIS IS A BAD IDEA.
MAYBE THIS CREATURE WASN'T GLIDING ALONGSIDE US, BUT HELPING US NAVIGATE?
ERIK IS RIGHT. SEVERAL SPECIES OF ANIMALS CAN ORIENT THEMSELVES AND NAVIGATE EFFECTIVELY ALONG A PLANET'S MAGNETIC FIELDS.
CLICK CLICK
...AND SINCE THE AFTERALL IS PART OF THE ELECTROMAGNETIC SPECTRUM... MAYBE WE'RE CLOSER TO THE UNSEEN CITY THAN WE REALIZE.
SOMETIMES THE THINGS WE'RE LOOKING FOR... WELL...

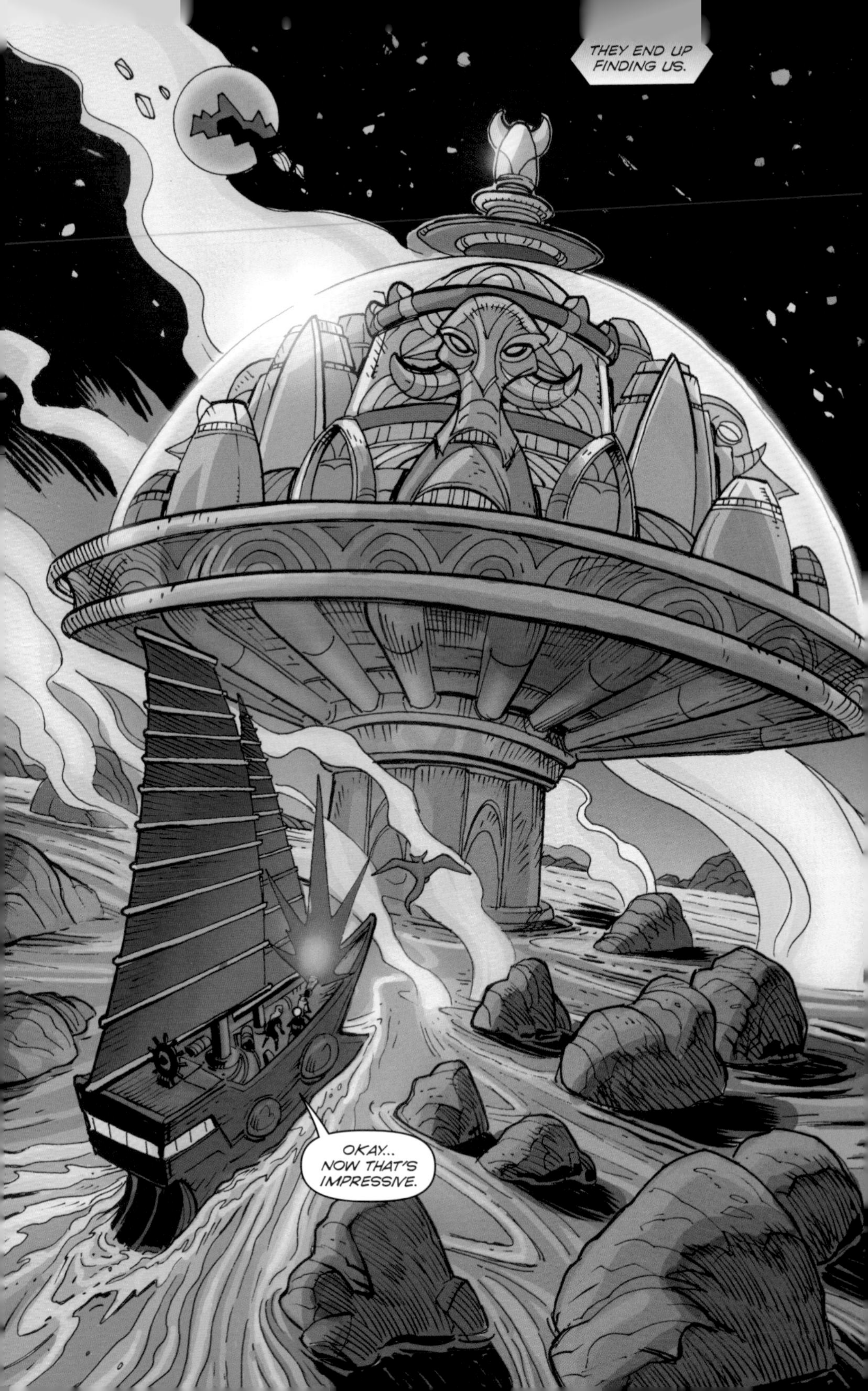
THEY END UP FINDING US.
OKAY... NOW THAT'S IMPRESSIVE.

WATCH OUT FOR PAPERCUTZ™

Welcome back to the beginning! Confused? Allow me to explain. I'm Jim Salicrup, the Editor-in-Chief of Papercutz, that gung-ho group of Earthlings dedicated to publishing great graphic novels for all ages. And it seems like every day I'm told that I've got a lot of explaining to do...

While this is indeed the very first THE ONLY LIVING GIRL graphic novel, it is also a continuation of the events seen in THE ONLY LIVING BOY graphic novel series. But if you're joining us for the first time, we hope you don't feel like you walked in on the middle of a movie and don't have a clue as to what's going on. It's a tricky balancing act–bringing first-timers up-to-speed without boring long-time fans–and writer/co-creator David Gallaher and artist/co-creator Steve Ellis did a wonderful job of pulling it off. They're cleverly giving you all the information you need to follow the story in THE ONLY LIVING GIRL without spoiling all the surprises still to be found in THE ONLY LIVING BOY.

What's THE ONLY LIVING BOY and why do I keep mentioning it? To further explain, THE ONLY LIVING BOY started out as a critically-acclaimed webcomic by David Gallaher and Steve Ellis, which you can still enjoy online at www.the-only-living-boy.com. Papercutz proudly published all THE ONLY LIVING BOY comics as a series of five graphic novels, and then collected those (plus even more comics) in THE ONLY LIVING BOY OMNIBUS. And so it seemed, the epic grand adventure of twelve-year-old Erik Farrell was brilliantly concluded and all nicely wrapped up... except it wasn't. All of which finally brings us to THE ONLY LIVING GIRL, the follow-up graphic novel series that begins where THE ONLY LIVING BOY ended. See, it all makes sense now.

For those of you who have been following along since the very first Papercutz edition of THE ONLY LIVING BOY, and are looking for even more great comics by the awesome team of Gallaher and Ellis while waiting for the next ONLY LIVING GIRL graphic novel, may I suggest a very interesting project I'm sure you'll enjoy–HIGH MOON. It's a supernatural western adventure, but it's not a Papercutz graphic novel suitable for all ages. It's like a lot of R-rated films that feature a lot of gun violence, such as *The Ballad of Buster Scruggs*. So, if you're not old enough to see an R-rated movie on your own, we strongly suggest either getting your parents' permission before looking at HIGH MOON or waiting till you're at least 17-years-old.

For lighter, approved for all-ages entertainment, fans of our favorite Mermidonian warrior-woman, Morgan Dwar, may enjoy the comical tales of someone who could possibly be her long-lost cousin–GILLBERT, "The Little Merman." Created, written, drawn, colored, and lettered by the super-famous, best-selling, and award-winning cartoonist Art Baltazar. Art is known for being the creative force behind *Itty Bitty Hellboy*, *Tiny Titans*, and so many more super-cool comics. GILLBERT #1 "The Little Merman" introduces us to Gillbert, the son of King Nauticus and Queen Niadora, and his friends Albert, Sherbert, and Anne, as they all party and deal with an alien invasion.

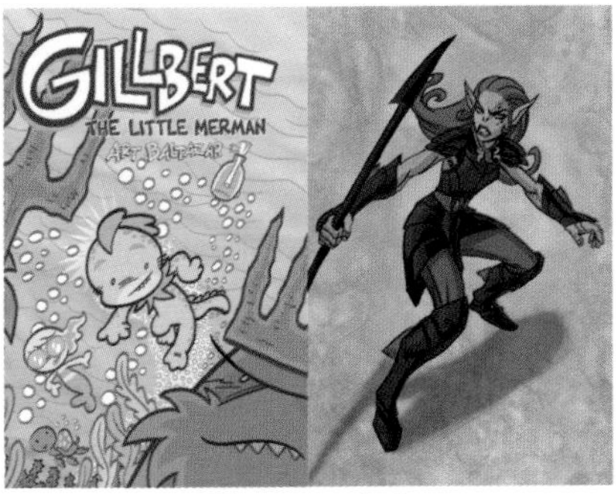
GILLBERT
THE LITTLE MERMAN
ART BALTAZAR
Distant cousins?

And let's not forget the classic tale by Hans Christian Andersen that originally brought us THE LITTLE MERMAID. Papercutz proudly presents a beautiful comics adaptation by Metaphrog (the award-winning duo of John Chalmers and Sandra Marrs), that David Gallaher (remember him?) describes thusly: "With exquisite illustrations and vibrant storytelling, THE LITTLE MERMAID is a fairy tale worth believing in." It truly is a beautiful book that we're sure you'll enjoy.

Which brings us back to THE ONLY LIVING GIRL #1, which if you enjoyed it as much as we did, you're now eager to get your hands on THE ONLY LIVING GIRL #2 "Beneath the Unseen City." It'll be available soon at booksellers everywhere.

Thanks, Jim

STAY IN TOUCH!

EMAIL: salicrup@papercutz.com
WEB: papercutz.com
INSTAGRAM: @papercutzgn
TWITTER: @papercutzgn
FACEBOOK: PAPERCUTZGRAPHICNOVELS
FAN MAIL: Papercutz, 160 Broadway, Suite 700, East Wing, New York, NY 10038